THE WASDALE MONSTER

W R Mitchell, a native of Skipton in Yorkshire, began a journalistic career on the *Craven Herald & Pioneer* over fifty years ago and shortly after joined Harry J Scott, founder of *The Dalesman* magazine, at Clapham, in the shadow of Ingleborough. For over forty years, he was closely involved in the editing of this world-famous magazine, being Editor for twenty of those years. For forty years, he edited its companion, *Cumbria,* and thus he knows the Lake District intimately. He is the author of over 100 books, mainly of North Country and Scottish interest, but *The Wasdale Monster* is his first work of fiction.

W R Mitchell

THE WASDALE MONSTER

Cover design by Ionicus

No story ever ends—it only
links the past and the future
from the film "Enchantment" (1948)

A CASTLEBERG PAPERBACK
1996

A Castleberg Book

First published in the United Kingdom in 1996

Copyright © W R Mitchell 1996

The moral right of the author has been asserted

ISBN 1 871064 89 9

Typeset in CG Times, printed and bound in the
United Kingdom by Lamberts Printers,
Station Road, Settle, North Yorkshire BD24 9AA

Published by Castleberg, 18 Yealand Avenue,
Giggleswick, Settle, North Yorkshire BD24 0AY

CONTENTS

Author's Note

For this light-hearted story of the Lake
District, I have pinched the name Wasdale and
its splendid setting. The people who inhabit
my Wasdale are imaginary. The reader is
unlikely to find their surnames in a telephone
directory; try a Cumbrian dialect dictionary
instead! I've simplified the Lakeland speech,
which at its most authentic soon makes an off-
comer feel like a daft dummel-heed.

1: Jonty Limps Home

Mist, grey and clammy as an old dish-cloth, draped itself over Wasdale, in north-west England. Wastwater was as uninspiring as yesterday's bathwater. Great Gable's striking pyramidical form was just a faint pencilled outline against the sky.

For once, Jonty Gill, one of the Wasdale postmen, had lost his chirpy manner. A restless little man, Cumbrian born and bred, he had a job he loved. He was paid good money for riding up and down the four-mile valley, for some brisk walking where a road was not quite long enough to reach a farm and for indulging in his favourite occupation—gossiping.

"Na then, Jonty—what's fresh?" said a farmer's wife as he sat by the kitchen table with a mug of tea in one hand.

"Nay . . ." he would drawl, sifting through the filing system of his mind for some up-to-date information.

And, of course, there was plenty of it. He reported on the progress of the latest bairn—and the health of t'auld folk. Willie Borran was "a bad colour". Bessy Nardus had fallen.

"Again?"

"Aye—again."

And so it went on. Gossip was the small change of life in Wasdale.

His favourite season was when gardens were fringed by the golden trumpets of daffodils and when the last streaks of snow ligged in the ancient joints of the mountains. Spring was always a little late up there. Later, the yellow effect switched from daffodils to the gorse bushes on the shores of Wastwater, which now had a carnival appearance.

In autumn, the hills were coppery with the dead fronds of bracken. And in winter, the dale (being just a few yards above sea level) might remain green while Great Gable and its retinue of high fells were iced over, like giant wedding cakes.

Wasdale, a bonnie lile valley, did not get rockier and steeper as the valley head was reached. It ended with fields as level as a dance floor. A scattering of white-painted buildings was linked by miles of drystone walls, plated with lime-green lichen. There had been so much stone to clear for farming that much of it had been piled up in damn great heaps.

Jonty usually had a cup of coffee in the kitchen of the hotel which had evolved from an inn kept by Will Ritson, the sage of Victorian days who claimed for Wasdale the distinction of having the tallest hill, the deepest lake and the biggest liar, which was himself.

The Postman had not been born in Wasdale but he had a good enough qualification to be counted a native. Some of his family had been buried in t'kirkyard. Until a trickle of incomers appeared, Wasdale was populated by a people of Norse stock, here by the right of a thousand generations.

Men hadn't a lot to say for themselves except when their tongues were loosened by some ale and they were in the mood to sing an old hunting song. The indomitable women of Wasdale held the families together and were as stay-at-home as the herdwick sheep, bonded to those parts of the fell where they drank their mother's milk.

The Wasdalers had known good times and very bad times, when they could do nowt else but curl up and go into a state of semi-hibernation. As Jonty told one of his Wasdale friends: "My grandad flitted three times—and he never owned more stuff than would fit on a handcart."

When times were good, the Wasdalers rejoiced with exceeding gladness, as the parson said in the lile church, one of the smallest in the land, where the congregation had to take it in turn to breathe and a tall man had to bend his head or risk bumping it against the beams. They, like the lile herdwick sheep, were said to have come from a galleon of the Spanish Armada, wrecked on the nearby coast.

As Jonty drove the postbus along the old familiar lakeside road on this depressing November day, he was irritated by the noisy swaying of the windscreen wipers. His eyes prickled with fatigue through the effort of trying to focus on indistinct objects. He narrowly avoiding hitting a sheep which in its greyness was only

8

one shade darker than the mist. The black-headed gulls, normally in a feeding frenzy, stuffing themselves with the bread and biscuits brought by day-trippers, were grounded.

"Bluddy heck," said Jonty, to himself.

He drew the postbus off the road opposite the fan-shaped Screes and reached into his bait-box for butties. His hands closed on—tomato sandwiches.

"Bluddy, bluddy heck!"

Jonty ate wet tomatoes in sodden bread while swaddled in mist of such liquid consistency it might almost be defined as drizzle. He looked towards the Screes, where a trillion pieces of rock were slithering towards the water.

At the stage where his morale was low, the Wasdale Monster struck. *Bang! Clatter!!* Jonty did not know it was a Monster, for the windows of his postbox had steamed up and resembled the frosted glass in the local chapel.

Bang! Clatter!! There followed the unmistakeable sound of a hub cap falling on to the road to roll for what seemed like minutes before beating a tattoo on the asphalt.

Jonty dashed from the bus in time to see a large shaggy animal moving into bracken cover. It had a rump on it like a hippo, but was covered by a gingery sort of hair. For a moment he thought he saw two red eyes glowing in the misty void between two banks of bracken. Then Whatever-It-Was had gone.

Jonty's immaculate postbus looked as though it had been butted by an elephant. On the shiny paintwork were several dinges and two indentations made by—horns.

When Jonty returned clatteringly to base with his badly damaged postbus, he didn't offer the usual sort of explanation, like being mugged by a drystone wall or being run into by a motorist who was admiring the view.

Jonty, driving into the post office yard amid a range of metallic sounds not normally associated with postbuses, said: "I was attacked by Summat Gingerish." Not surprisingly, the other postmen laughed.

It had been very Big. And it had a Ginger Hue. That's all he remembered. One minute, he'd been supping thermos-tea and minding his own business. Then—WHAM!

Jonty now played the "if" game. If it hadn't been drizzly; if

9

the windows hadn't been steamed up, and if— Charlie Hawkrigg, a tall, pale-faced chap with grizzle-grey hair and the weary manner of a professional who has seen it all, emerged from his supervisor's office and gave a six-inch yawn. "Get on with it, lad, or we'll be here all night." (He actually said aw neet).

As a story-teller, Jonty had never done better. And Charlie had known him long enough to recognise the symptoms attending a badly shaken-up postman. Jonty normally had a good complexion, as though he'd been rubbed all over with red rudd, the stuff used on Lakeland sheep at showtime. Now t'lad was a sort of creamy shade.

Charlie reached for an accident form and said: "Tell me more..."

"There's not a lot to tell. I hadn't been so scared since I kept just ahead of Marmy Divvent's bull."

"And..."

"The postbus is slightly damaged. Not much, mind you..."

"And..."

Jonty thought for a moment, then a cloud passed over his face. "If I don't get home soon, my missus will fair skelpt me." Fear of being skelped kept many a Cumbrian male to the straight and narrow track. Millicent was a waspish woman, with a tongue so long, it could wrap itself round both sides of an argument. Jonty had a recurring nightmare concerning his relations with his wife.

He dreamed he had drifted up to Heaven, listened to the heavenly choir, had a chat with an angel who'd lived in Ulverston—and was then told (not told) by St Peter: "Sorry, lad, we've made a mistake. Thou's come up here too soon. We're sending you back to your Millicent." He'd wake up in a cold sweat.

Jonty had made the mistake of telling Millicent about his dream, one evening, after he'd had a little too much to drink, they were getting ready for bed, and she seemed to be in a pleasanter mood than usual. She had been getting undressed— beside the window. The curtains had not been drawn. Millicent simply said: "Don't be so bluddy daft."

They had lapsed into their usual grumpy state. Jonty, still fortified by ale, told his wife: "Close them bedroom curtains.

10

Or switch off t'light. I don't want folk thinking I married you for your money."

(One story's good till another is told. What Millicent thought about Jonty, which was not much, was relayed to the "girls", her friends of the Sewing Circle, at their weekly meeting in the Vicarage. They had all nodded their heads, understandingly).

Jonty snapped out of his reverie. Charlie Hawkrigg was still waiting for details of the accident and the damage to the postbus. Old Tom, who eked out his pension by washing down post office vehicles, pointed to where the postbus had been dinged or scuffed. And one of the hub caps was missing.

"Bluddy hell!" he said. Churchgoing Tom exceeded himself, for normally he went no further than "Heck" or, perhaps, "Bluddy Heck!" Or even, when t'vicar was present, "Rose-red Heck!" Tom tried to lift the nearside door back into its normal position. A squeal of tortured metal had replaced a satisfying "clunk"...It was definitely a bloody-hell situation.

Owd Tom thought for a moment or two, as was his wont, and said: "Thoo must have bin struck by yan o' them low-flying jet airyplanes. One nearly took me cap wi' it when I were fishing. It came so low ower t'lake, yon pilot must have had to spit out a mouthful of watter."

Jonty stuck to his story. The Thing had desecrated the title on the van side and ROYAL MAIL had become ROYAL MA. Part of the Royal Crown had been obliterated by the assailant.

Charlie, briefly jocular, said: "I don't think t'Post Office recognises Summat Gingerish. We'd better put down 'Large Unidentified Creature'." He didn't quite manage to smother a laugh.

Jonty let his colleagues have their say, then pointed to the top side of a really big dinge and the unmistakable horn marks.

"By heck," said Charlie, "thoo's been attacked by Old Nick himself."

Old Tom pulled a tuft of ginger hair from a crack between a wheel and its hub cap, which was now somewhat awry. The old chap sniffed at it and pronounced that the hair had an oily tang -as well it might, seeing where it had been lodged.

Tom looked at it closely, then pronounced: "It's summat like the hair of yon barmaid at *Shepherds' Rest*."

11

Jonty exploded. "You can leave barmaids out of this. I'm going home."

As the Good Book says, the day was far spent. Jonty lived a few miles from Wasdale. To get himself in a right frame of mind to face the wife, he drove on the fell road. The mist had thinned. Beyond the soft green of the coastal strip, and the duller green of the marshes, lay the sea, normally grey as old pewter but now salmon-pink from the afterglow of a newly-departed sun. That blue-grey smudge on the horizon was the Isle of Man.

The news of Jonty's encounter spread up Wasdale with the speed of a Reuter's news report. When Grannie Tyson, of Dale Head, heard the tale, she took to her bed and wailed: "It's the Wasdale Monster, come back to plague us all. The last time it was here, it killed fifty sheep. And a cockerel. Killed 'em just for devilment! My old Dad said it lived in a gill, up Sty Head way, and chewed up rowan trees when there was nowt else to eat."

Grannie, now into her nineties, had shrivelled till she had to be propped up with half a dozen cushions. Her face had so many lines on it she resembled an unsteeped prune. Grannie's nearest and dearest shook their heads sadly. T'owd lass was delirious again. But they were all nice to her. She was said to have a fair amount o' money tucked away. And when she died, she'd have to leave it all behind. There are no pockets in shrouds.

By teatime, Grannie Tyson had regained her good spirits, also her seat by the fire—and her finicky appetite. "I'm partial to be bit of ham," and hey-presto it was there before her, with some lettuce, a slice of cheese and some home-made brown bread.

Frank Gribble, the mole-catcher, heard about Jonty's exploit as he tidied up after another successful campaign against the little furry critters which, as he was never tired of telling folk, can be stroked both way because the hair sticks straight out. "Otherwise they wouldn't be able to go ahint (reverse)."

In moments of stress, Fred (like many another dalesman) called upon the old god Heck. After giving an update on the local moles, he said: "By Heck, I reckon that if a mole grew till it was ten feet high, it'd scare the living daylights out o' folk. And it could drill its way from Wasd'll to Ennerd'll."

Jonty the Postman returned to his round in another postbus. He no longer parked it just across from t'Screes. He wasn't one for tempting fate. Jonty was also a bit nervous of hairy things. He had been since he encountered Jake Hullet's new dog. Jake's wife shouted across t'farmyard: "It won't hurt you. It wags its tail." Then she dashed off. The dog made straight for Jonty, displaying all its teeth.

Just as he thought it would take a chunk from one of his calves, t'auld dog appeared, grabbed it by one ear and held it down till Jonty reached safety—and a nip of whisky, taken as a medicine, of course.

"Just think," said Jonty, to himself, "yon Monster I saw was at least six times as big as Jake's dog."

2: Owd Jack

The "lads" who gathered in the bar of the auction mart on the following Thursday had no doubt about the cause of Jonty's accident. He'd been supping too much yal, as they called ale in Cumbria. Or 'appen he had taken too much whisky and too little watter.

It was a newish auction mart, made largely of breeze blocks and corrugated zinc. Slam a door shut and five minutes went by before the echoes stopped. T'auction dealt with stock from up to twenty miles away.

In the old days, cattle had stood in the main street of the town. Dealers with sovereigns jingling in their pockets haggled for them. Now everything was under cover. Sovereigns had given way to cheque books. In attendance at the mart, in addition to farmers and dealers, were retired men with nowt better to do with their time than stare at cattle and sheep they'd no intention of buying. Then, finding staring hard work, they slipped into cafe or bar for refreshment.

13

Jonty's close encounter with a strange beast was discussed in the auction mart bar by hardened drinkers and those others who sipped and played dominoes until their eyes were too weary to focus on the white spots.

Simeon Upshaw, a florid chap with a brewer's goitre, was not one to act on his own advice and remarked, between sips: "If I saw Summat Gingerish, I'd take an asprin—and it'd go away!"

A titter went from farmer to farmer, along the ale-sticky bar, which at that moment was decked with whisky glasses in various stages of being emptied.

Some farmers took their whisky neat, some took it with watter. One man—heaven forbid—diluted it with lemonade. "Who'se supping whisky and pop?" demanded Jake Thomas, with his usual verbal delicacy.

When no one was looking, Jack Smithson—born and bred a Methodist—used his tot to water a handy geranium. "I don't want a red nose," he said.

Jake replied: "Nawther do I, so I'll keep on drinking till it goes blue."

A bar was a place where you paid good money to forget your troubles. The place fair crackled with witty comments. Bert Foomart exploded with laughter at the remembrance of a recent conversation between Jennie and Sarah, who were neighbours down Millom way.

Jennie told Sarah that her lad had been seen drinking whisky.

"Nay."

"Aye."

Sarah looked upset. She asked: "Was it neat?"

And Jennie said: "Nay—it were broad dayleet."

Simeon reckoned that the Postman's Monster had escaped from a wildlife park. "Doon south, it's usually a puma. Up here, it could be a bear—or summat."

"Appen it's a chap from t'Inland Revenue in disguise," remarked Bert Foomart, before switching the conversation back to summat sensible—like fat stock prices.

It was a busy time at t'auction mart, in the echo-chamber of the sale ring, which had a high roof with skylights so that the mint-sucking farmers and dealers could see what they were doing and the company didn't waste a lot of electricity. The decorations

14

were few—just one or two posters, announcing future sales, blue-tacked to the wall. The menu for the cafe included the item "Plumbs and Custard".

Fat lambs, a few at a time, were going through the ring. Tom Ruddock, the auctioneer, sat at a rostrum which looked a bit like a pulpit. He had a head on him which was craggy, like the popular idea of an Old Testament prophet. His voice cut through the babble of talk with the high-pitched intensity of a pneumatic drill.

Tom was a Methody preacher who, when leading the Flock in extempore prayer, sounded so much like an auctioneer that he might have ended the prayer by slapping the rostrum and shouting "Gone!" instead of saying a respectful "Amen".

Tom Ruddock knew all the dealers. He knew some of them too well and was alert to the individual ways of bidding. There was Ted Wunter, surreptitiously scratching his nose. Jake Kebby was playing wi' t'neb of his cap. Raynor Bumley simply winked. Everybody made a fuss of Raynor. He was buying stock for t'Co-op.

A mixed bunch of farmers, watching the proceedings with kestrel-clear eyes, missed nowt. There was Simmy, outwardly gormless-looking, but with a mind as sharp and keen as a computer. Johnny Jack related to identical twins. Because no one could tell one from t'other, the names were run together.

The dalesmen were inclined to be leaner and darker than t'big blond chaps from t'low country between the high fells and deep big blue sea. Up in t'dales, you had to tie a couple of blades of grass together to stop 'em going back into t'grund. In the low country, the land was 'growy'.

"How's ta goin' on, lad?"

"Aw reet."

"Thou doesn't look it."

"I git a bit on my sheep and me wool."

"And?"

"There were a bit on some spuds."

"Cheer up."

"Nay—I were just thinking how much all that has taken out of t'ground?"

Every farmer was a character—his own man. They were still

15

laughing about Sam Hullock who was so used to getting grants and subsidies in the old days, when someone mentioned income tax he said: "I haven't drawn that yet."

Cloth caps were popular. At the mart, the nebs were worn at the front, not the back, signifying the men were off-duty. Most of 'em were here for a day off, or a natter with retired farmers, men who'd finished-up in lile brick bungalows at edge o' town and kept getting under their wives' feet.

The men talked about tips and yows and hoggs. They guffawed when the latest, somewhat smutty tale circulated.

It was about the annoyed husband who had a row with his wife and stomped out of the house shouting: "And you're no good i' bed!" Later, he felt guilty at what he had said so he rang up home. A few minutes elapsed before his wife answered. "What's ta been doin'?" asked her husband. "Nay," she replied, "after what you said about me being no good i' bed, I thought I'd get a second opinion."

No one had seen the Wasdale Monster. Or anything gingery, except a dun cow at Hill Top. And that hadn't looked very aggressive.

The farmers commuted from sale ring to cafe. Smiles like rays of sunlight on a snizy day were to be seen as a clattering sound heralded the arrival at the mart of everyone's favourite character, Owd Jack, a master of the art of looking and acting daft whenever it suited his purposes.

Jack was driving an old Fordson tractor he'd bought off t'War Agricultural Committee after the last war. If you looked carefully, you might see flecks of orange—the original paint. Otherwise, the tractor was two-tone, being orange and rust. This trusty vehicle had not spent a night under cover since it arrived in the district under a haze of exhaust fumes. Where there were no moving parts, tufts of grass grew in the ingrained muck.

Jack also had an old Land Rover. When he just missed colliding with the doctor's car one morning, the doctor said that if Jack didn't give up driving he'd have his licence taken away from him.

And Owd Jack had replied: "Thoo'd have a job on. I haven't got a licence."

Jack was tall and so lean his bones looked like scaffolding. He

16

sagged only at the shoulders. His father had, like many another dale father, nearly worked the lad to death. Jack had become a legend in his lifetime for an astonishing feat, performed in the *Woolsack* one Merrie Neet. He supped a welly-ful of ale.

He'd taken his time, of course. And he hadn't been much good after that. In short, he passed out. When he began to recover, about one o'clock in the morning, they had propped him on his beloved Fordson and dispersed into the night. Next morning, Owd Jack was still there, on his auld tractor. He was snoring. There was a film of dew on his forehead.

Jack, who wasn't really a Wasdaler (for his grandmother had been born in Ennerdale, in t'next valley) was generally accepted to be a queer old stick. When he stopped wearing his false teeth, his face collapsed in the middle. He was a bit of a loner, though convivial enough if he met another farmer, especially if t'other chap paid for t'drinks.

Jack was forever jacketless, with shirt sleeves rolled up, even in the middle of winter. The thing you best remembered about Jack was his gummy laugh. Some people got him to laugh simply to see his shining, toothless gums.

Years had gone by since the last of his teeth had been yanked out. It was a do-it-yourself job, for Jack hadn't a raw nerve in his body and he didn't like to bother t'dentist. If anyone asked him how he coped, he usually replied: "These gums are so hard, I can crack Brazil nuts with 'em."

Not many people had visited Jack. Nor had they seen his farmstead, which was tucked away in a corrie. This was Jack's Little Kingdom. It lay off the official footpaths, though inevitably one or two ramblers came this way. Which is why he usually had a lively young bull about the place.

Jack lived in an old farmstead, stone and slate, with a big circular chimney. Years ago, the outside had been kept painted white. Now, it was no more colourful than the big lichened boulders round about. Inside, it was little better than a cave, with a flagstone floor and a slopstone instead of a sink. He was one of the last to retain a big kitchen range, which was fireplace, oven and hot-water boiler in one and (in this case) cried out for another application of black lead.

Owd Jack's barn was air conditioned—through a hole in the

17

roof. An old stable was used as a hen house. Circumstances had led to the breeding of nimble hens, able to get under cover before the teeth of the fox closed around them.

Owd Jack had no wireless. No television. He went to bed when it was dark. He awakened as the morning sun illuminated his bedroom. From the moment he set foot on the floor, he was active, busy, determined to wear out rather than rust away. Jack lived for work (or wark, as he called it). He could never resist a bargain. In an outbuilding were a dozen toilet seats which had been going cheap at a sale of bankrupt stock.

He used to have one or two cows. When one of them was receptive, and a bull was needed, he would set off with her, in t'middle o' t'neet, to use one of his neighbour's bulls—without asking him, of course. On a calm night, the owner of the bull, sleeping fitfully, might hear nothing more than the sound of a latch on the farmyard gate and the joyful lowing of the cow when the job was well done.

As Jack said, what are neighbours for? By cockcrow, his cow was back on the farm with the nearest thing to a bovine smile on its face.

"Owt fresh your way?" asked one of his cronies at the auction mart.

"Nay," said Jack, "nowt except yon blonde, big bosomy lass 'at keeps plaguing me." He wheezed several times and for a moment seemed about to choke. No one rushed to perform the (disagreeable) task of giving him the kiss of life. In any case, Jack was nobbut laughing.

Another of his old pals had asked him what he did about sex. Old Jack replied: "I brews missen a cup o' tea at that time."

"He's a caution," said the lass behind the counter in the auction mart cafe after he'd given her a wink.

Jack wanted to know about Jonty's accident with the postbus, which he saw daily—a red blob on the dale road far below—as he tended his sheep.

"Jonty says a big animal ran into it."

"Aye."

"Thou doesn't seem surprised."

Owd Jack gave another wheezy laugh. "Nay, it's more than likely he ran over a yard-brush!"

18

And that was as much as they got out of Jack before he opened the back of his big, old-fashioned, disreputable trailer. A Herdwick tup clattered down, scattered one or two bystanders, bounced off a metal railing and stood defiantly with vapour emerging from its nostrils. Jack, waving his hands and shouting in his curiously high-pitched voice, managed to get it penned.

"You've got to give Jack credit for knowing a bit aboot breeding. I've never seen better sheep. I think he must winter 'em in t'parlour." The speaker was Isaac Tyson, from Wasdale Head. That day he'd been putting a few beef cattle through a separate ring, sniffing with disapproval as their weight was assessed in kilos.

"Bluddy Common Market!" he grunted to his neighbour at the ringside. "We'll be having garlic wi' everything afore long."

Isaac had the long, lean, greyish look of an updale farmer. He wore a cloth cap at all times except when he was in bed. He never mastered the art of putting it on straight. The neb was always off centre. Otherwise, he was unmemorable, blunt-featured, walrus-moustached and with eyebrows which had a hedge-like bushiness about them.

He limped a bit, as well he might, having once been kicked by a horse. "Just 'od this," someone had said, when he was nobbut fifteen. He was handed some reins. The horse was a Clydesdale, which towered above the lile lad and had saucer-shaped feet which, when it brought them sharply down, seemed to make the dale ring. Those were the days when there'd be hundreds of horses at the annual fair.

Isaac was joined by a young woman who, by her good looks and virility, turned the heads of everyone in the cafe. She was slim, not too tall and wore her dark hair short. She moved with a sprightly gait and had a brisk way of talking.

"By, lad, but thoo's kept this a secret," said Simeon, who had drifted in from the bar.

"Doesn't thoo recognise her? She's our Jane, whose just passed out as a vet."

"By Heck! She doesn't look old enuff to have left school."

Jane, now twenty-four, joined a local veterinary practice straight from university and still carried herself and her bag of tricks self-consciously. She also had a mobile phone.

19

"Is that so thoo can ring up t'office for advice?" Jane had been brought up among farmers. She knew how to handle their ribald talk. And she knew about livestock.

"Have they thought up any more diseases?" asked one farmer.

Isaac retorted: "If thoo doesn't shut up, she'll be slapping some 'lastoplast on thy busted nose," he said, in an unusually aggressive manner.

"Eh, Jane luv, but it's good to see you again," said one of the waitresses who was called "Miss" despite her wizened face and grey hair. "Pop in and see us sometime. Dan's bin supping sheep med'cine agean."

"Miss" turned to shout into the kitchen: "Sausage and chips, twice." And Owd Jack couldn't resist shouting: "She heard you first time."

Apart from the old lass, the auction mart cafe was staffed by lile lasses wi' print pinafores. They served coffee to a few and good strong tea to most.

Where Jane went, Tony was not too far behind. He was tall, athletic, Nordic—and fearfully possessive. He'd been reared by a widowed mother who doted on him. He had been at school with Jane and fought her battles. Isaac Tyson had given him the farm man's job. He always regretted it but hadn't the heart to get rid of him.

Tony was stronger than the proverbial ox, glorying in his strength. He hadn't got round to ripping up telephone books for show because he thought such a thing was daft. He lifted a herdwick tup over a stile for a bet.

Tony was still at Dale Head, sleeping in t'lile room over t'porch, where if he stretched out full length, the top of his head and soles of his feet and both hands were pressed against the walls. There was not even enough room for a piece of lino.

Tony was present at every meal, with his seat by the fire on every long winter evening. He was heartsick when Jane was away at university. If he thought she'd as much as looked at another man, he would have snapped his back as though breaking a piece of dead wood. No one liked to see Tony riled.

He took it for granted that he and Jane would be wed one day. They had not even held hands, though there had been the odd peck on the cheek at party games when they were young. Tony

20

dare not make the move in case he was repulsed, cast into outer darkness.

Jane, not so far having met anyone who suited her, and not wanting to upset Tony, was content to leave the situation as it was. It drifted on. No other man in the valley would lay a finger on her unless they felt that they could beat Tony, the big tough man, in a straight fight.

Isaac despaired. "I don't know why you bother with 'im when there's better fish in t'sea. He's a nice enough lad, but you were made for someone better, lass."

Jane then felt sorry for Tony.

At the auction mart, Isaac was proud to show off his talented daughter.

Another farmer approached them. "Eh, lass—is that red Ford thine?"

Jane nodded.

"Well, there's a chap inside. He's got a tinny voice. Keeps saying: 'Base to Vet Three.' It's a funny do."

Jane walked briskly to the car.

"Vet Three to Base. Vet Three to Base. Over."

"Base to Vet Three. Complications with a calving cow. Lane Head."

"Vet Three to Base. I'm on my way. Over."

The farmer who had approached Jane about the disembodied voice shook his head and remarked: "Well I never..."

Jane drove off, enjoying the sensation she was causing at the auction mart, which was mainly the preserve of men. And Tony's eyes bore into her like gimlets as she departed in a haze of exhaust fumes from the car's diesel engine.

Now the dominant sound at the mart was the rumbling of stomachs. The movement to t'cafe of farmers, a few wives and some kids—almost all of them in wellies—became something of a stampede. Some people went in for a plateful of hot food. Most farmers, somewhat frugal in their ways, and with evening meals in prospect, had snacks. Typically there was a Door-Stopper, a big, triangular ham sandwich (brown bread, of course) and mini-Kit Kats, two pieces instead of four, wrapped up in foil with the familiar red label. Whatever did farmers do afore somebody invented Kit Kats?

21

Owd Jack stuck to Door-Stoppers—literally. He never was a delicate eater. He'd once tried some trifle but denounced it as "ower many tastes at yance". You knew where you were with ham sandwiches. And by eating 'em you were supporting t'British farmer. Wasdale men had long since divided humanity into two—Farmers and Others.

Isaac Tyson, who was honour-bound not to buy a Kit Kat, said: "My wife's a regular weight-watcher. And it's my bluddy weight she watches." He sighed at the memory of gargantuan fry-ups, then turned to Simeon and remarked: "What's up with us, these days? My grandfadder started every day supping a basin full o' warm fat. He died in t'hayfield. Aged ninety."

3: Up T'Dale

Wasdale opens its mouth to mild breezes sweeping in from the Irish Sea. Jonty, the Postman, drove a replacement postbus up the valley on a breezy day when dry leaves were chasing each other, when washing was smacking itself on lines at the farmstead and the ravens were being blown about the sky like charred fragments from a November bonfire.

On his way to work, Jonty had seen with something of a shiver the cooling towers of the nuclear power installation at Calder Hall and Sellafield. They looked like giant milk bottles on the Lakeland doorstep. His grandfather had told him when Sellafield was just the name of a Cumberland farm. The farmer grew oats, reared fine cattle and wintered young sheep from the dales. Now there was all this high-tech, atomic stuff, with wires strung all over t'place.

God knaws what they make there, thought Jonty. He couldn't

lay the blame on t'atomic place for the fact that the sheep of the west got a dose of radio-activity and gave t'needle of a geiger counter St Vitus Dance. A shower of rain got mixed up with radio-active fall-out from Chernobyl, somewhere in Russia.

There was nothing to worry about, of course. But people still worried, even when they got cramp. Whatever it was couldn't be seen. Or felt. You'd no idea what was happening to you. A sick joke went the rounds—that the farmers had got rid of their dogs and when "gathering" sheep on the fells they carried geiger counters.

Jonty, who simultaneously loved and hated the science fiction films shown on television, imagined some mysterious It emerging from a bubbling sludge north of Ravenglass to dominate the world. That is, if t'County Council would let it!

Jonty relaxed as he parked the postbus outside the office in the lile town of Brimly. The digital clock on the car dashboard showed 6.00. He slipped into his working jacket and headed for the sorting office.

When Charlie was in a teasing mood he was like a heat-seeking missile. Tha couldn't shak him off. "I had thought of putting a few old tyres down either side of this new vehicle, but t'garage hadn't got any to spare."

The postbus was due to leave at 6-30. Jonty, brooding about the Monster, was watching the digital clock jerk its way to that time when a young man with a rucksack appeared.

He hardly needed to open his mouth for Jonty to recognise an American. He had a chequered shirt, tight fitted denims and opened up the conversation with a drawling "Say..." Jonty had a cousin in Detroit. He always began a sentence like that.

The American asked: "How many dollars—er—pounds is it to get to Jack Smirthwaite's place?"

"You mean Owd Jack's! It's thirty new pence to you!"

"You sure do have some quaint expressions here."

Jonty said: "Most of yours were exported from England by t'Pilgrim Fathers."

The American held up his hands, as though warding off a blow. "I surrender..."

"Sit down, lad—an' shut up!"

But first impressions were favourable. This American wasn't

23

yan o' t'bragging sort. He was a big chap and gangling, clean-shaven and, for an American, quite modest. He spoke crisply but not in that high-pitched monotone, as heard on television, when each person seemed to have a megaphone stuck in his/her throat.

His tall, loose frame lolled across the two front passenger seats. His features were John Waynish and would doubtless turn the head of any cinema-daft English lass he encountered.

"Have you come all the way from America with nobbut a rucksack?"

"Say, how come this word 'nobbut'?"

"It means 'only'."

The American smiled and replied: "All I nobbut need is a clean shirt and a few dollars."

Jonty said: "Thou's larnin'. Nobody's axed for Owd Jack before. He's a bit of a recluse."

The American laughed. "I don't really want Jack. Only his cottage. A friend told me about it. He stayed for a couple of nights. He said it was like something out of one of those old black-and-white English films. All cobwebs and ghosts. Sounds swell. All I want is a bed and desk. I've a writing job to do for my degree back in the States. I thought I'd come back to the Old Country. And find out what you folks do with your lives."

You'll be popular, thought Jonty. Most people tried to keep their private lives, well—dark. It wasn't easy. When Fred the farmer's son "ran away" with that servant lass from High Dodd, the news reached Wasdale Head in a couple of hours. And a friend who worked for t'Council said the couple living at the Old Vicarage had different surnames. So had the three kids. That set the gossipers clacking."

"You sure do talk funny," said the young American. "I'll need an interpreter."

Jonty laughed. "Owd Jack'll tell thee about t'local way o' life. Especially how to tickle a trout, gaff a salmon, cure mutton, snare rabbits—and that's only a start. He lives ower t'hill, oot o' sight of t'valley. You can only begin to wonder what he gits up to."

The postbus headed out of town, between hedges busy with clattering blackbirds, which had been gorging themselves on thorn berries. Soon the hedges gave way to walls...

24

"Say, tell me something about those cute stone fences. . . ."

The scenery was now on the grand scale.

"What a gorgeous hunk of landscape," said the American.

Jonty introduced himself. "Jonty Gill."

The American said: "My name's Henry."

"And your second name?"

"Don't laugh. Its Kilkoff."

"Sounds more like a medicine."

Added Jonty: "You're not going to have a dull moment up here with a name like that."

"Say something in dialect," said the American.

"If thoo knaws nowt, say nowt; if thoo knaws summat, say less."

"Say, what does that mean?"

Jonty smiled and replied: "Keep your bluddy mouth closed."

The postbus began its daily grind, up the gear box and down the gear box, along the dale road, over little packhorse-type bridges, to the first stop at the postbox outside Washolme, the big house by the lake where liveth Major Riseley, late of the Army. More precisely, of the Stationery Corps.

Riseley had a high opinion of himself. He was classified by the locals as high society, "yan o' t'nobs", a position achieved through being Director of the Swartz Trust, which owned the upper dale, with the exception of the Tyson farm.

Jonty thought that Henry—er—Kilkoff (titter titter) showed a special interest in Washolme and its principal resident. Personally, it gave the postman the creeps. It was a big, solid slab of ancient masonry which, of an evening, was a-flicker with bats. It was said to be haunted by two ghosts—a headless man and a dog, who walked from the big house to Dog Hill, though how the man found his way when he had no head had puzzled Jonty since his boyhood, when he first heard the tale.

Henry remarked: "It's medieval."

Said Jonty: "It's bluddy draughty."

Henry plied him with questions about Washolme and the major. Said Jonty: "There's only one chap stands up to Major Riseley and that's Isaac Tyson. He owns his own farm. It's not part of the estate."

And there was trouble brewing between the Major and the

25

Farmer.

No one seemed to know much about The Swartz Trust except that it had been established by a hyperactive American Grannie who had a five day European tour during which she spent several hours at the head of Wasdale. She had thought the place was "cute" and, having a few million dollars to spare, she bought it up.

Within the dale, landowner after landowner had fallen to the allure of money—lots of money. Only the Tysons—and more precisely Grannie Tyson—held out. She'd never forgiven the Americans for taking the Colonies off us! And Isaac, a traditionalist, was fighting a rearguard action to keep foreign influences out of his native Wasdale.

Eleanor Swartz, having bought the place, couldn't decide what to do with it. The local opinion was to "leave well alone". She met Riseley in a London hotel, which he had been visiting for no more reason than to have afternoon tea with an old Army pal. He was delighted to get the job of Director of the Swartz Trust, even though he—quite literally—had never travelled north of Watford.

He had discussed the matter with his wife. This meant he told her what he had in mind.

"Where's Wasdale, dear?"

They got out a motoring guide, but that wasn't much help. A friend in a Ministry took him to a map-room where England was displayed on a moderately large scale. By the time he had located Wasdale he was standing on a step ladder. Wasdale seemed just a notch on the western side of the Lake District.

To Major Gerald Riseley, the big house, the extensive grounds, a staff of servants and a local community, however sullen they might seem, represented Achievement. In the South Country, gentlemen of his rank were two-a-penny. Majors were not high enough on the social scale to be invited to open fetes.

Riseley's wartime battles had been fought in the secretarial division. He had won a campaign over paper-clips. He earned renown, if not a medal, when he held up a battle for two hours because all the necessary forms had not been completed.

Betsy, his wife, who had been reduced to the proverbial bag of nerves by her husband's nagging, had one real pleasure in life, and that was to see him come a cropper. She had a nervous

26

chuckle whenever her husband lost face, as he frequently did without knowing it. He lined up the workmen for inspection at the start of each working day. He posted up daily orders in the house and once commented on an excessive use of soap. "Wife please note.".

It was she, not Riseley, who usually met Jonty at the postbox and handed him items of mail which wouldn't fit the slot. Sometimes she got on the bus—a little mousy woman with a sketching pad and some pencils. It was amazing how she warmed to friendship and how those little solitary jaunts did her good after days, sometimes weeks, in the big house, with only the dogs to talk to.

This morning, it was Riseley himself who came blustering up to the bus. "Here, my good man . . ."

Jonty thought to himself: "I'm not your good man. I work for the post office."

"Postman. Make sure this packet is not damaged while in your custody."

Jonty thought: "It'll be my pleasure to jump on it when we're out of sight."

The Major peered at the American as though he was examining a rare species at a cage in the zoo.

Jonty said: "Major—may I introduce . . . Oh, I'll let our visitor do the introduction."

"I'm Kilkoff."

"I beg your pardon."

"Kilkoff."

The Major retired in confusion, to Jonty's delight. A conversation with Major Riseley was full of clipped comments. It was like playing verbal ping-pong. Jonty glanced at the address on the packet, as the Major hoped he would.

It was addressed to Prince Charles at Buckingham Palace.

Within a few hours, everyone knew about it. The general presumption was that the Major had invited the Prince to visit Wasdale. Perhaps for the Show. And perhaps . . . On its way round the parish, this rolling stone of a Royal story gathered the moss of imaginative story-telling.

The Wasdale which Henry saw on the early stages of his way up the dale had been wrapped in dove-grey twilight. When the

27

sun cleared the high fells, the American beheld a glorious upsweep of land. On the lower slopes the breeze was running a comb through a mass of bracken which was as bronzed as if it had been taken for a fortnight's holiday by the Mediterranean. The lake shore was a jumble of big rounded boulders and odd stretches of shingle. There were promontories, feathered with gulls.

Henry noticed the rowans, standing to attention on the fellsides and beside the becks. Each held out arms full of berries as red as—er—a postbus. "Gee—there's some goats."

"Them's herdwicks—native sheep. They've all got white faces. Dark brown 'uns are hoggs—they were lambs last spring. Grey 'uns are t'older sheep. They're a bit bony, but I've tasted nowt better than herdwick mutton."

The rocks were like the bare bones of the landscape, protruding through the skin of the earth. Wastwater was so blue that Henry wondered if someone had poured a few gallons of ink into it.

Beyond were the fan-shaped Screes. A lile cloud was drifting by them, as though trying to find a way round. Two gulls argued over a crust of bread.

Yewbarrow seemed to block out half the sky. The American's keen eyes picked out the multi-coloured form of the first fell-walker of the day, fly-like in size on a worn trod so steep it looked as though it had been propped against the fell.

Then Great Gable came into view—big, triangular, with a redness about it as if the mountain was bleeding.

A herdwick ewe, intent on licking the last traces of salt from the road, where it had been spread in icy conditions last winter, was banished to the bracken by Willie Braithwaite's collie dog, normally a pillion passenger on his "quad", his go-everywhere vehicle. "It's gitten a funny name—all-terrain vehicle, or summat," he said. "It's terrible noisy, but better than walking. There's only one thing wrong—it wasn't med in England. Can't we mak owt these days?"

They chatted, with Jonty in the bus and Willie still straddling his four-wheeled thingamajig. The dog curled up on the pillion seat.

Willie was a lile chap, wearing his old cloth cap—wi' t'neb to

28

one side—but otherwise swathed in waterproof clothing, with wellies on his feet. "Ah's going to t'vet for some medicine. Some of me sheep's coughin'."

Of course, he'd heard about Jonty's damaged postbus. Said Willie: "What hit you?" And Jonty told his tale once again.

"Gingery?" queried Willie, not expecting a reply. "Well that's a funny thing..."

Willie needed five minutes to get his story together. It was almost as strange as Jonty's. "Yan or two hikers arrived at t'farmhouse one neet and asked if they could sleep in t'barn. They aimed to stay on t'tops and watch t'sun rise ower t'hills. Townsfolk have some daft ideas. But summat turned up."

"Summat?" It was Jonty's turn to talk.

"Aye, summat." Willie pushed his cap to the front of his head and stretched t'back of his head, as though trying to coax out t'rest of t'story. "They yammered on about going for a walk at t'edge o' dark and coming back to where they'd pitched tents to find 'em in shreds, and all their clothes and food and things scattered to t'four winds."

"Nay."

"Aye—and that's all I know, except that they were drip-white when they turned up and they were still white, and not wanting any breakfast, next morning when they set off home. I don't knaw what else'll fit except thy 'gingery thing'."

Jonty handed Willie a tax demand, in the traditional buff envelope. That shut him up. The Postman continued his journey up the dale. Now the few buildings of Wasdale Head came into view, held together by miles of drystone walls. And there was t'lile kirk, behind its herdwick-proof walls and with a yew tree for company.

Henry Kilkoff, the American, had his vision of Lakeland Loveliness. "Gee!" he said. And he was not thinking of the landscape.

The postbus moved slowly, in deference to sheep and Land Rovers being operated by men with restless eyes, dividing the time between looking at the road and checking on their farm stock.

Twenty yards from the road was a parallel path. And along the path strode a young woman. At first glance, she looked like a

29

fragment fallen from a rainbow. The effect was created by a red anorak, yellow jumper, blue jeans and boots. A collie dog ran its zig-zag course, reading the morning newspaper composed of various delicate scents.

Henry let out a wavering whistle at the sight of a lithesome figure and a bonny face edged by dark hair, with high silver highlights from the morning sun.

"Whose that lovely creature?"

"Keep your eyes off her. It's Jane Tyson. She's spoken for, as we say in these parts. Leastways, there's an understanding that t'farm man's bahn to wed her. And her father is as protective as an old yow to its latest lamb. Won't allow anybody strange near her."

"Poor thing."

Jonty winked. "She's a spirited lass. Browt up among farmers. Browt up to hard work as well. Now she's all high-tech. You know, radio and mobile phone. She goes for a walk every morning with her dog. She lost her phone one time. I'd to ring the number when I got to t'nearest telephone box. She heard that phone peep-peeping in the heather."

Jonty waved at Jane. She returned the compliment. The dog, venturing down to the road, cocked up a hind leg against the postbus.

As the vehicle moved ahead of Jane, Henry was left with a tingling sensation. It was not lust but love at first sight. Unmindful of the impression she had created, Jane strode on, with a springy gait, through a tousled landscape sparkling with raindrops which had caught the eye of the morning sun.

Jonty swung the wheel of the postbus. Now its bonnet was angled towards the sky as he followed a track. For several minutes, it ran through a sort of grey paste—the effect of water on the quarry-bottoms which had reinforced the track.

The bus was stopped in a turning area. Henry was directed to a gate and a track going on, meandering between ranks of firs. "That's it, lad."

The postbus departed. Henry, his mind still coloured by a vision of Jane, blundered along the path, getting wetter at every footfall as those bejewelled fronds jettisoned water. He arrived in a glade where stood Owd Jack's cottage, a substantial

30

building, of stone and slate, standing on an outcrop of rock. An owl, which had been sitting on an outjutting piece of slate, with its body pressed against the chimney, flew away like a big brown moth.

"Merry hell!" said Henry to himself, as he prepared to take possession.

Jonty, continuing on his postal rounds, had a "crack" with Isaac Tyson, farmer. "Now what's ta bin dooin'?" asked Isaac.

And, of course, Jonty had to tell the tale again.

You've already met Isaac Tyson at t'auction mart. Then he was clean-shaven, except for his moustache. Now, neglected, his face sprouted hairs which were as tough as a yard brush. He only shaved when he went to the auction mart—or when Florrie, his wife, telled him to. Most of the farmers at the dalehead had beards. Some of them ran the risk, at dipping time, of being chucked in the trough with the sheep.

Said Jonty: "I'm that sick o' telling t'tale, I think I'll put it on tape and lend it out."

Isaac prepared to enjoy his first smoke of the morning, ramming black twist into the bowl of his pipe. He sucked and coughed alternatively until there was a cherry-red glow. A wisp of tobacco rose in the still air. Isaac's dog, sensing much talk, settled down, closed its eyes and began to chase imaginery sheep across the high pastures of its mind. Soon it tired of that game. From the dog came—snoring!

There'd been Tysons in Wasdale since t'Vikings were here. Or so they said. So many Tysons had been buried in t'kirkyard they'd had to take some muck out to put more Tysons in. Or so they said. The Tysons were sheep farmers. Isaac's grandfather, Herdwick Ben, was yan o' those who smartened up t'breed last century.

Isaac Tyson, not being a fancy talker, simply remarked to Jonty, when his tale was told: "Ah bet thou'd bin on t'bottle."

Jonty did not reply. He handed over the mail to Florrie Tyson, who ruled the household and was forever hovering in the background with sheets of newspaper, ready to put them down on her clean floors if Isaac decided to enter the house without the formality of taking off his big boots. Isaac used to say (when Florrie wasn't there): "If we'd lived in a city she'd have polished

31

the tram lines."

Klonk! It was November. Tupping time. A dull thud signified to Isaac that two of his herdwick tups (which by rights should have been in separate fields) had met, head to head, with a force which left one of them reeling. The victor, which was the animal "playing at home," shook its white head and stood on legs as stout and firm as those on a kitchen table.

It was a truly impressive tup, its wool still bearing the red rudd which Isaac had put on for Wasdale Show, a week or two afore. Each tup had its harem of about fifty yows, but now and again there was a footloose one which covered its own yows, then invaded the territory of another. Two tups, glaring at each other, were a fearsome sight. In Wasdale, it was not just the yows which had headaches.

"There's your answer," said Isaac. "Thou were hit by a tup." (He actually used the word "tip", which is the way in the west of Lakeland. In the east, where they've more spare time, they say "twearp").

The Monarch of Tyson's Farm, fattened up by good summer grazing and having grown a new hairy coat after the clipping, was strutting, having banished the last competitor for the favours of the females.

The hint of a smile played round the ends of Isaac's mouth. "Wastwatter isn't Loch Ness. It hasn't eneuf room for a Monster. Tha's been attacked by an auld tup."

Said Florrie: "If you two don't git on wi' some work—you'll be attacked by me."

Tyson strode to where his two best tups were glaring at each other, ready to resume battle—to clash, horn to horn. Isaac must try and part them before there was trouble. He had to do it carefully, having lost the end of one finger, nipped off between two horns, when he was young and feckless.

Jane arrived, with her old car and crackly radio. Isaac's face, on which one might normally bend iron bars, softened perceptibly. So did Tony, who had been tidying up the outbarn.

Jonty thought: "There's going to be some trouble when that lass takes somebody's fancy. Tony just isn't her type."

The Monster of Wasdale struck again during the night. Isaac Tyson, up early, for his mother always said a person died i' bed, brewed himself a pot of tea, not yet aware of the overnight drama which had occurred a couple of fields away from the house.

He roused the fire from its overnight slumber and (as was his wont) made some porridge in his little brass pan. When he'd transferred the porridge to a plate, he let t'dog clean up the pan. He never mentioned this custom to Florrie. To her, cleanliness came before godliness, the former being a daily occurrence and the latter once a week, when she went to the morning service at the little church.

Isaac Tyson joked to his friends that he got up early and took his wife a cup of coffee, stirring in a tablespoonful of Epsom Salts, so that she'd not lig in bed when there was work to be done. In fact, he treasured his quiet hour, up by himself, with only the collie dog for company.

It ended when Grannie Tyson, now ninety years old, rapped her walking stick on her bedroom floor and demanded attention.

The hot spell of weather had ended with overnight rain. Isaac sniffed the air appreciatively. Rain kept the fields green and gave the becks a voice. The only snag about rain in Wasdale was that when it started it never knew when to give up!

Isaac donned his waterproofs, laced up his boots, took down his workaday crook from hooks against one of the gnarled beams and whistled up his dog. Normally, everything was quiet. This morning, the yows were bleating anxiously. He didn't have to open the first gate because it had been lifted off its hinges and whatever did it had broken one of the bars as it crossed the recumbent gate into the next field.

The herdwick sheep, proud little sheep, didn't like being bunched up. Now they were gathered in a corner of the field, looking distinctly uneasy. A gap had appeared in a wall which yesterday looked as though it still had fifty years of life in it. Something—maybe even a JCB—appeared to have trampled on it. "Now what?" said Isaac to his best friend—himself.

With a mounting sense of foreboding, the farmer walked through the fog-grass and then found his best tup—not up and alert, as it should be at tupping down, but down and quite dead. Mangled, its neck broken.

Tyson's dog was petrified with fright. Then it began to whimper. "Come here, lass," said the farmer. But that was the

33

last thing the dog wanted to do. It went off to the farm, pursued by Isaac Tyson's choicest swear words.

Jane's special training as a vet was not necessary in this case. She recognised death when she saw it.

4: Medical Matters

We left Henry Kilkoff as he strode down the path to Owd Jack's cottage. He walked briskly, humming to himself, intoxicated by the scenery. Bracken and birch and the purple spires of foxgloves flanked the path. He inhaled the tang of moist soil and wet vegetation. In gaps between trees he saw the fells, in shadow, like pieces of dark paper stuck against the sky. They impressed Henry by their size and form. Here was unspoilt scenery in miniature.

He rounded a corner—and beheld his quarters for the next few months.

"Gee!" said Henry, to a passing crow.

The condition of the building seemed to lie somewhere between ramshackled and wrecked. There was a roof, but some of the slates were awry. The roof was supported by four solid-looking walls. The windows held panes which spiders had covered with webs. These were now as dense and grey as muslin.

The portal was low. Henry's face struck it, breaking his glasses. Blood flowed from a cut over the eye. He staunched it with his handkerchief.

On the door was a good north-country sneck. When Henry pressed it, the sneck refused to move. He applied more pressure. The clonk roused the echoes in the rooms beyond and brought a round of chacking from a pair of jackdaws nesting in the chimney.

There was but a single room, with a lile kitchen stuck on as though it was an afterthought. The room was furnished (as promised) but with a collection of objects which competed with each other with regard to age and dereliction. The deal table had a wobble. From the kitchen came the unmistakable sound of a dripping tap—just one tap, presumably delivering only cold water. The sink was cracked.

Amazingly, there was electricity, so the loss of the chimney to the jackdaws would not be too serious. He might use the electric fire—if it worked.

Owd Jack arrived. His appearance did not surprise Henry, who had heard the throbbing tractor as it came down the lane.

"Na, then," said Jack, slipping his cap to the back of his head and scratching his forehead, as though to induce thought, "you'll be reet comfortable here. . .I've browt you a sleeping bag. T'last chap who took t'place left it and didn't leave an address."

"How do I warm water?"

Jack replied: "There's nowt like dowsin' thissen wi' cold watter for getting t'blood circulating in a morning. And it's a poor stomach 'at can't warm up a cold drink."

"I might want some coffee."

"They serve a luvly cup at the *Woolsack*."

Jack pointed to a corner of the room. "There's a besom ower there. I bowt it off a witch." The old man chuckled. "I'll dump thee a load o' logs for t'fire next time I'm passing. But think on—get all twigs out o' t'chimney afore thoo lights a fire. Otherwise thoo'll have t'place alight. Now I mun be off. . ."

"Is there a doctor in the valley?"

"Aye, lad. Is ta poorly?"

"Blood pressure."

"I'm not surprised, sort o' life thoo leads out in America. I watch a lot of films on t'telly. It's bedlam over theeer. . ."

". . .and I hit my head on the doorhead. There's a deep cut. I'd better have it seen to."

Jack found a plaster in a box left by a tenant. He advanced on Henry and stuck the plaster in roughly the area of the gash. Another piece of plaster was handed to Henry.

"Stick that on t'bridge of thi spectacles," he commanded.

And off went Jack, in a haze of pipe smoke and diesel fumes.

35

Henry set off for the village. His gait was less buoyant now. With his head throbbing and a lump the size of a duck-egg forming, he was in a self-pitying mood. The bracken and the birch and the foxglove had lost some of their lustre.

The "walking wounded" of Wasdale met at the surgery, which was the front room of Mabel's lile cottage. Mabel, who was referred to as "Miss" by the respectful patients of Dr Dykie, made both the front room and the passage available, three times a week. It was possibly the only surgery in England with pot-dogs on the mantlepiece, antimacassers on the couch and a picture of *The Death of Nelson* on the wall.

It was tough luck if you ran out of medicine on Tuesdays, Thursdays and at week-ends. But at other times Dr Dykie was available. He was an approachable man, "yan of us". He was a working class lad made good who, to his credit, didn't act posh, tended to go around in oldish clothes and in wet weather put on an old mac which had lost its belt, the successor of which was a length of binder twine.

The doctor used Christian names, even with patients he was meeting for the first time. Not letting such things as surgery hours govern his life, he had been known to stop his car by a meadow at haytime, to clamber over the wall and tell one of his patients to bare his chest while he "sounded" it. He regularly arrived at the dalehead, pipped his car horn and waited for the local geriatrics to turn up to have their stock of pills renewed.

Grannie Tyson said he was turning all the senior citizens into drug-addicts, and she had so many pills her bones were operating on ball bearings.

Her good friend Florence said: "T'littliest pills is t'strongest. Them lile sulphur things are so strong they could knock out an elephant."

Henry arrived just in time to hear the word elephant, which he could not equate with a quiet valley in westernmost Lakeland.

An ancient man, who had retired from farming years before, recalled when it was all bottle-medicine, and you had to shake the bottle before pouring out a spoonful; he said: "At least, you felt summat was doing you good." More than one man resorted to sheep medicine (or whisky, applied both externally and internally) in an emergency.

It was not easy to gossip at the surgery, for the chairs were set in a line, right down the passage, twixt the door and Mabel Seed's aspidistra—the one which was borrowed whenever the local drama group was putting on a play with an old-fashioned setting.

Henry occupied the last chair and shamelessly listened to the nearest conversation.

"What's up?"

"Nay, I felt under t'weather."

She got no further before the other lady cut in. "My husband's got back-ache. He often has when there's some really messy job to be done on t'farm. I first checked that he hadn't got his braces crossed, which happened yance afore, then I thought I'd come and make an appointment to see t'doctor...Appen when he's cured that, he could graft on some brain-bumps. He's lacking a bit o' sense."

"Wouldn't it be best to let your husband come himself?"

"Nay. He'd nivver get right tale. And he couldn't be seen coming here when I told everybody he had backache, could he?"

"Where does he get his pain?" asked her friend, anxious to know whether it was high up or low down.

"He gets it in pig-oils. When he's bending down."

"Oh."

"Aye."

The inner door opened. A doleful patient shuffled off, as though expecting the next appointment to be for a post mortem. The bell rang. Next-in-line entered the surgery, while the rest exchanged chairs, rather like musical chairs without the music.

Jonty was the next person to see the doctor. He asked for a tonic. All he wanted was a chat. They call it councilling these days. It had been quite traumatic to have an unidentified object wrecking your postbus.

Dr Dykie was sympathetic. "Have you got any pains?"

"Aye. There's one here, another doon theer, and a third in me stomach. That's worst o' t'lot."

"Are you a worrying type?"

"Well, t'missus says I worries a bit."

"Good. Cheerio."

37

"Do I get owt to swallow?"

"Jonty—it's delayed shock. Go and have a pint with the lads. Or run up and down Gable."

"What do I tell t'wife? She telled me to stick out for some medicine."

Dr Dykie scribbled out a prescription.

"What this?" said Jonty, who prided himself on reading bad hand-writing but could not work out what the doctor had written.

"Water tablets. Just one dose, mind you. And don't stray far from the toilet or trees."

Out in the passage, two ladies were conversing. One was doing most of the talking. "I went to yan o' t'young dentists t'other day. Folk say he's brilliant. I complained about one of me crowns. He rived it off. Left a sharp stem. And me mouth seemed full o' granite."

"Nivver."

"Aye. I went back to see him. He said: 'Shall I file 'em doon?' I said: 'Tha's done enuff, lad. Give me back my crown. That telled him'."

Jeff Lollard, looking drawn and pale, hadn't slept a wink for a night or two. "T'doctor gave me some anti-summat to tide me ower t'week-end. I was in agony. He said it were polypuses in t'bladder. Nowt sinister, mind you. But could you sleep wi' polypuses?"

"What's polypusses?"

"I don't know. And I don't want to know. I'm going to tell t'doctor I just wants 'em shiftin'."

Two chairs away, a woman spoke in sleep-inducing detail about her visit to the Infirmary for some plastic surgery (to her nose). "It were a Greek doctor. I asked him how they said 'no' in Greek. He telled me. Then I asked him how they said 'yes' in Greek. He telled me. He asked me why I wanted to knaw. He shouldn't have needed to ask. If I was stuck there with 'im fettlin' up my nose and if he asked me if I was in pain, I'd want to be able to say 'yes' in Greek, right quick, afore it got worse..."

"What's up wi' thee, lad?" Simeon was talking to Henry, who had sunk into a cottage-induced stupor. What on earth should he do about it?

"There must be summat wrang wi' thee."

"Pills," said Henry, entering into the dale spirit of sharing troubles. "Blood pressure pills." To himself he said: "I'll sure need some strong ones before I'm through."

Henry got his pills.

Simeon, who had fallen, broken his spectacles and (like Henry) suffered a bleeding gash above his left eye, was not in the doctor's presence for long. He left sticking plaster on the spectacles and closed the deep wound above the eye with some super glue, observing: "When you feel it smarting, don't move your head. Or it will be stuck to my finger for the next week or two."

5: Shepherds' Meet

The Wasdalers were usually a bit morose on the doorstep of winter. With tales being told of a raging Monster, farmers began to take to the fells in two's. Bevies of wives travelled by car to the shops of Whitehaven. Children were told not to go near any strange animals, especially gingerish ones.

It was a dale under siege.

When the Shepherds' Meet took place at the *Woolsack,* the dapper, moustached, nicotine-stained John Thwaite dispensed pints to the natives—and made up all sorts of fancy drinks for the touroids.

John, a Mancunian who was looked down upon because that city had connected its cold water taps to the Lake District, was "too smart by half", as Isaac Tyson said. "Yon chap likes to top t'stack." For the benefit of one of the visitors, it was quietly explained that if someone told a tall story, John Thwaite would tell an even taller one. And if someone had just bought a new set of cards, John was able to produce the latest novelty, a shuffling machine.

If John had lived in the Lakeland dale country for a little longer, he would realise that no one is allowed to put on airs; that the bragger is quickly cut down to size. Mine-host of the *Woolsack* had installed a row of wall lights, to create a romantic atmosphere. They didn't give a lot of light. So one of the Wasdale farmers demolished the system. Blundering about in semi-darkness, he reached for the light switch, which was at the end of a piece of flex, and instead of pressing the switch he yanked the fitment off the wall. A short-circuit made the light even dimmer.

The brass-framed stable lamp, picked up in a Carlisle junk shop, hung from a beam in the bar until it was removed on safety grounds, having plucked the cap from almost every man in the dale. So the *Woolsack* reverted to what it had been since the beginning of licensing time—a country pub, with flagged floors, iron-framed tables, padded benches and stools as hard as t' Devil's forehead.

John Thwaite had improved the toilets, which were now incorporated in the main building. In t'auld days, there were two sentry-box like structures oot at t'back. One door was marked TUPS and the other YOWS. He'd left the old signs on the doors because at least one a week in summer a visitor took a photograph of them and they were printed in newspapers and magazines. Any sort of publicity was good.

The toilet paper used to be the previous week's edition of the *Cumberland Gazette,* the pieces strung together at one corner and dangling from a rusty nail. Now the *Woolsack* toilets had become the talk of the dale, being accommodated in an extension to the pub, with walls covered by white tiles and a wash-basin complete with one of those blower-things for drying your hands. Willie Braithwaite said: "It's either cold—or as fierce as a blow-lamp."

John Thwaite used them frequently, if only to admire yet again the feeling of well-being imparted by the latest gadgetry. Then, one evening, in what the farmers still called the "Tups" section, he encountered one of the bearded, unwashed climbers who infested the dale. He was warming up a can of soup on a portable gas-fired stove. Henceforth, an unguarded back door to the pub was kept locked.

The Shepherds' Meet was a November event which used to precede tupping time, for it was intended as a meeting place for farmfolk who had taken up stray sheep and now returned them to their rightful owners. Each year, the old, old stories were told of the Lakeland farmer's capacity to sup ale. No one quite achieved Owd Jack's distinction of imbibing a welly-full but in the old horse and cart days a farmer invariably left it to the horse to find the way home.

Lile Ernie, whipper-in to the Hunt, had a tale of a chap who called when he was already market-fresh. Someone took the horse from the shafts, turned the animal round and slipped it back into the shafts. The boozer, staggering from the *Woolsack,* stared in disbelief and was heard to say, slurringly: "Howsh this 'oss manished to chuck a cart ower its head?"

Nowadays, when everyone had a telephone, it was a simple job to inquire about sheep and regard the Meet as a dark-day social event, with singing, a hotpot meal—and much boozing. The farmers met at a time when visitors, including the hikers with shredded tents, had migrated with the swallows to their winter quarters, far to the south.

The dalesfolk had the dale to themselves. For a few weeks, the old way of life re-asserted itself. It was just as well there were not many ultra-sensitive urban visitors around because t'Hunt arrived. Tom Shunner, the huntsman, had several 'couple' of hounds (never call them dogs) which Lile Ernie, the whipper-in, controlled—mainly with his tongue. As Tom said: "Lile Ernie does t'main o' t'work. He's t'chap 'at gits oot on t'tops."

For, as you will have gathered, the Lakelander hunts on foot, not on horses. In the old days, they hallooed to each other—a sort of Cumbrian yodel. The sound raised every echo between the pudding basin-shaped fells. Now the men were in touch with each other by short-wave radio. "Tally-ho, tally-ho. Over and out . . ."

The Wasdale Hunt killed about a hundred foxes a year. No one stopped to consider how it managed to do this, without making savage inroads into the number of foxes. A stranger who

41

suggested it was just on an expensive cull of what Nature would have done, left to herself, would be advised to wear his best running shoes.

The Hunt pursued foxes as a sport. It usually got the very old and the very young animals. It had been so for ages, ever since hunts were announced by someone standing on a tomb in t'kirkyard after morning service. John Peel had cheated. He rode a pony, named Dunny, on the big fells back o' Skidder.

Fox-hunting, a dalesman would say (if he bothered to talk about it) was part of Lakeland's heritage. And so, more to the point, was imbibing copious quantities of ale, with—now and again—a nip of something more concentrated.

A tremor of excitement—number six on the John Peel scale—was detectable in Wasdale on the day of the hunt. The huntsman had a jacket of what the Men of the Shires called "hunting pink". It was red. The hounds looked half-starved but lived royally at the kennels, which were doon at Dale Foot. A touch of hunger kept them active.

The anti-hunting lobby (a little chap from Whitehaven) usually finished upside down in t'beck. Undaunted, and wearing waterproofs, he was present next time the Hunt assembled.

Mine-host of the *Woolsack* was his usual mournful self. In summer, he complained there were too many visitors. You couldn't stir for 'em. In winter, there was not enough trade to keep flesh on a crow.

Which was why he had a special welcome for Henry Kilkoff. He had not been seen for a week or two since his arrival in the dale, but the local grapevine indicated he had been visited by a variety of tradesmen who had been given instructions to repair Owd Jack's cottage till it was inhabitable. And Henry had learnt a good Cumberland word—fettle, to fix.

Henry settled comfortably into the life of the *Woolsack*, usually turning up in the evening, having the odd pint of ale, commenting on the warmth of the liquid as compared with the tongue-tingling drinks of his native land, and then questioning anyone who would talk about local life.

Henry Kilkoff had a mission—to record. His interviews were punctuated by the word "gee" so as not to disappoint the dalesfolk. One of them remarked: "By heck, lad, but for a Yank thoo's not so bad!'' Praise indeed!

One magical evening, Jane arrived, alone. She'd been attending a difficult calving and wanted a strong drink. She called it dram-bustin'. When the whisky had put some fire in her, she walked across to Henry and said, affably: "I hope that old rogue Jack's not plucking you."

"Plucking?"

"Taking too much of your money."

Henry, intoxicated by the near presence of this lively, vital young woman, lapsed into an embarrassed silence. She laughed, swept out of the inn and left Henry to his fantasizing about a life shared with Jane Tyson. Every day ended with a glowing sunset.

Henry, not knowing how people dressed for a fox hunt, was clad in his brightest, patterned shirt and skin-tight trousers.

Jane, who was forever flitting up and down the dale, attending to her veterinary duties, suddenly breezed into Henry's life again. She was with Tony. Henry sauntered up to the huntsman with his tape-recorder. Hunty said: "Don't bother me just now, Yank. Thee get into t'cigarette line."

Henry joined the spectators. He contrived to stand next to Jane and gave up when the ever-faithful Tony stared at Henry with the intensity of a lazer.

Timmy Sourthwaite was the first to return. He didn't look very pleased. "We've lost two or three hounds," he said, before wrapping his left hand round a pint of ale.

"Tha shouldn't be so bloody careless," said mine-host.

"Nay," gasped Timmy, "they're lost for good. Dead. Stiff. It were on that brant hillside beyond Middle How. T'pack went into t'bracken. There was a hell of a scrap. Most of t'hoonds limped out. But summat attacked 'em and two lay dead. And don't tell me t'fox turned on 'em."

Timmy's story was born out by the Hunt supporters. "There's summat funny happened on yon fellside," said Timmy.

Mine-host said nothing. (Actually he said "nowt"). He wasn't going to be the first person to mention the Monster.

For once, nobody had the heart to sing the old hunting songs. The party broke up at the ridiculously early hour of 2 a.m.

Henry cadged a lift most of the way home. He blundered along the path. The bare branches of trees were waving about like

43

wizened fingers. An owl hooted. At the door to his cottage his fingers encountered something soft. He lit the paraffin lamp, pumped it up and held it up.

Someone had tacked the bloody corpse of an animal to the door.

Henry shuddered. Was this a hint for him to quit the dale? Was he showing too much interest in some of the local people?

A piece of paper was held against the door by the corpse. He held up the lamp—then laughed.

It was a message, in Owd Jack's writing: "Here's a hare (he spelt it hair). Summat for t'pot."

6: Last Rites For Grannie

It was a quiet winter, during which the Monster seemed to hibernate. The fells were powdered white with snow. The herdwick sheep, brought down in good time, spent a few weeks in the big flat fields of the dalehead. The summit of Great Gable was packed with folk. Sandwich paper flew around like confetti.

Henry set about studying local heritage, trying to sort out history from hysteria. He liked the story of Wilson's Horse, a rock said to be as big as St Paul's Cathedral which slithered down the Screes into Wastwater and caused a tidal wave twenty foot high. There was Moses, who distilled whisky without the blessing of the Excise men, and supply gentry and parsons. If they could see no harm in it, and wanted his goods, then he was willing to oblige them.

Meanwhile, at the Tyson farm, Grannie spent her last days on earth tormented by tales of the Monster of Wasdale. She wanted a daily report. Her agitation was reflected in the brisk movements of her old rocking chair and she would spend much time tut-tutting or, in her squeaky little voice, saying: "Count your sheep!"

On days when there were no reports of the Monster, her rocking chair stood inactive. Once, after being still and quiet for a couple of hours, Grannie Tyson beheld at the assembled family—for it was her birthday—and said: "Don't look at me like that! I'll outlive t'lot of you."

She asked for Jane. "You're a good lass. When I've gone. . . ."

". . . don't upset yourself, Grannie."

"Count the sheep!"

She closed her eyes.

"Has she gone?" asked an indiscreet niece who, even when whispering, had a voice that carried across the dale.

"No, she hasn't gone." It was Grannie talking, with her eyes still closed.

There had been one or two false alarms. Two relatives, living in Borrowdale, heard she was fading fast and, realising they had nothing good to wear for her funeral, decided to visit Keswick to buy some more clothes. They alerted a Keswick friend and said they hoped to call and see her. When they had not arrived in a fortnight, the friend rang them up. She was sorry to have misssed them. "Nay," was the reply. "We didn't have to come after all. Grannie got better."

Eventually, she died peacefully in her sleep. She who had been a big bonnie woman had shrivelled up with advanced age till there was next to nowt of her. As one of her nieces said: "She were ready for off."

Someone sent for t'undertaker, who when he had attended to Grannie was persuaded to have a cup of tea. He sat there, beside the fire, looking intently from one to another. As each person came under his gaze they felt a deathly chill passing through them.

Early the following morning, the news of Grannie's death was telephoned to the Vicarage.

The Methodists had "niver git into Wasd'll". The Anglicans held sway. Representing their interests and having what the Victorians had quaintly called "spiritual oversight" was the Vicar (the Rev Eric Bisky). He had a particularly hectic time, his

45

oversight extending to four big parishes. As he said: "I've got to run to stand still!"

Carol, the vicar's wife, had left him. There was no row. One day she announced: "I married you. I've had three children by you. I've washed and cleaned for you. Now it's my turn to enjoy myself." And, buying some student clothes—old jersey, jeans—from an Oxfam shop, she sauntered forth to resume the academic life.

Carol was so thin that when she had a cup of tea she looked like a thermometer. This city lass had never quite got the hang of dale life. In his unChristian moments, Eric Bisky was glad she had left. She had tried to stir up militant feminist ideas in the Mothers' Union. She had made a bid for chairmanship of the Women's Institute.

The bid failed when she had given a talk about Jerusalem. This turned out to be a line-by-line condemnation of the famous lines written by Blake. "Jerusalem" was sung at the start of every WI meeting. Carol said they should choose something cheerful and leave "Jerusalem" to the last day of the Labour Party Conference.

In his wife's absence, the Rev Bisky coped as best he could in a spacious, underfurnished—oh, so remote and lonely—Victorian Vicarage in which the echoes chased each other. The only well-furnished room was his study, a high-tec study, so high-tec that one visiting parishioner, his lower jaw drooping at the sight of computer and fax machine, imagined t'parson must have a direct line to the Almighty.

One of his problems at Wasdale was trying to find room, in a much-crowded churchyard, for Grannie Tyson. The family plot was full. Grannie, overhearing someone talking about it, had said: "Don't make a fuss. Just scatter mi ashes on t'top."

It was a good funeral, as funerals go. The whole dale seemed to be represented, the men wearing crow-black suits, though the normal serious expression was replaced by one of joy. For, after all, Grannie Tyson had "been spared" for well over ninety years. When she was ninety, and grumbled about her "sciatics" and "poor old legs", someone pointed out that she was still better on her feet than she had been ninety years before.

The church had pew-space for fifty. Early last century, as

46

Henry's researches showed, there were but two pews, plus some sheep forms on trestles. No door was to be found. The entry was blocked by a thorn bush. It kept sheep out of the building, which was bedded with bracken, like a stable. Provost Fox had referred to Wasdale Head at sheep-shearing time as "a congregation of smells".

Henry joined the seventy or so people who stood outside, saying nice things about Grannie, though she had been a bit of a tyrant. The vicar read the Twenty-third Psalm. Grannie had always liked the idea of being led through green pastures, though if they were owt like those at her neighbour's farm they could bide a bit o' good muck.

Henry, arriving late, stood beside the yew tree and heard the melodious dale voices singing a last farewell to Grannie. He saw the neat hole, in a corner of the graveyard, which would be Grannie's last resting place and the start of another Tyson patch. The grave-digger had cut through some of the tree roots. A neat pile of soil lay to one side.

The parson intoned: "Dust to dust, ashes to ashes."

Henry saw Jane, wearing black, and Tony, in his best setting-off suit, with a shirt bulging at the neck. He stayed protectively close to Jane, who scarcely needed protecting. Already, in her veterinary career, she had been butted and stamped on by cattle and bitten by the spoilt Dalmatian of one of the "new settlers", as Isaac called off-comers.

She smiled at Henry. "I hope you'll come along for something to eat and drink before you go home." Then she was off, on family duties, consoling the old aunties and telling the dale farmers to be sure to go to the *Woolsack* for coffee (or summat stronger).

Said Amos: "I bet there'll be some o' them lile three-sided sandwiches which taste as though they've just been stroked wi' ham." Amos, was forever concerned about the state of his stomach.

Isaac Tyson, forgetting for a moment his bereavement, smiled and said: "Thoo always was a good trough-er".

It was the first time Henry had entered a real old Lakeland farmhouse. There was slate everywhere—forming a simple porch over the door and, in gigantic slabs, covering the ground

47

floor being in turn covered, here and there, by home-made rugs, made of the family's cast-off clothing, cut into strips. They looked pretty.

Hooks were set in the ceiling àbove the big old-fashioned fireplace. "Them's for dryin' t-pig meat," said Amos. The low beams were decked with prize cards from Wasdale Show, and a good many cards were red, testifying to Isaac's first-rate stock.

Henry was ushered to a wicker chair, across the back of which was draped the fleece from a black sheep. He was handed a cup of tea—the best china!—and found himself under the unblinking stare of the stuffed head of a fox. The "brush" dangled from the wooden mount.

Henry shuddered.

"Which part of America do you come from?" One of Jane's aunties had borne down on him. She was wearing black. Her face was a contrasting white.

"New York."

"I've never been any further than Manchester."

"You're sure lucky. I've seen nowhere prettier than this Lake District."

Auntie purred.

"Have you got a girl friend?"

Henry, despite his age and massive build, felt a rush of blood to the capilliaries of his face and his scalp prickled at the directness of the question.

"No, auntie." Jane had come to the rescue, bearing down on them like the Cavalry in a Western movie. Jane added: "He's too young for you. Go and find someone you're own age."

There was no rancour. The two women kissed. Auntie was directed towards the only remaining bachelor of her generation.

"Keep off Jane," hissed Tony, who—emerging from the throng—blocked the only approach to Henry until it was time for the company to disperse. Tony grunted: "She's my girl."

"And a very nice girl, too," said Henry, affably.

The look on Tony's face indicated that he had made at least one enemy in Wasdale.

Grannie's funeral was the last great social event of the year. The winter was unusually quiet. The Hunt would be back in spring, when foxes started worrying some of the new lambs.

Everyone mourned the loss of the hounds and Isaac Tyson's cur dogs helped out in the war against foxes by going off on their own and killing a few.

For those who did not care for crowds, which meant the most discerning of fell-walkers and climbers, wintry Wasdale was a dreamland of gleaming white fells set against an azure sky. The dale was not far above sea level, and snow did not linger long, but the fells—sweeping up to over three thousand feet—were like gigantic iced wedding cakes. Who needed a Christmas card when there was so much real beauty all around.

At the *Woolsack*, mine-host and his wife (a timid lass called Christine) and son Jamie (a holy terror) went through the daily ritual of washing the flagged floor with no special expectation of it getting dirty during the day. John and Christine were chatting one evening when Christine (who normally only spoke when she was spoken to) said: "We'll have to advertise...."

"Never!" said her husband.

Half an hour went by in silence.

"What about Loch Ness...?"

John grunted. His wife was raving again. Loch Ness!"

Mary was the typical cowed wife. On this occasion she ventured a word: "Monster!"

Of course! Publicity! Hipe! Public Interest! Visitors! Brass! Mabel Seed, the newspaper correspondent, had just included a note in the Wasdale news about an albino carrion crow. A Monster was much more newsworthy.

That night, the Monster stalked John Thwaite in his dreams. He thought of it as a big black hound, with eyes as big as saucers and teeth like those on a saw. Then he imagined it to be a monster like Nessie, which periodically crawled out of Wastwater to head-butt the cars of innocent motorists. (For it must be pretty monotonous living at the bottom of a lake for centuries).

It was a taut and trembling John Thwaite who visited Mabel's lile cottage. She was completing a report on the week's whist drive. Mabel could be summed up in one word: "Homely". As homely as a pair of slippers beside the fire. She was forty-fivish but dreadfully old-fashioned. And she had no news sense. Her whist drive report, which would rate no more than three lines in the *Cumberland Gazette*, had a three-decker heading, each line

49

underlined in red. The report extended to five lines and included the winners, first "ladies", then "gents". She attached her news items together, at the top left hand side of each page, in her own distinctive way, sewing them with needle and wool—usually red wool.

Mabel had heard of the Monster, of course. She said she would include a few lines about it, but it might take a week or two to persuade The Editor there was a monster. It was a month before he used the piece about the albino carrion crow. Mabel had to get a farmer friend to shoot it. She sent the corpse along with the report, which she had re-written—in the past tense.

Indeed, Reg had not been pleased when he found a crow's body on his desk. Especially as, as he looked, it was vacated by a battalion of red mite, in close ranks.

Several days after Mabel Seed reported on the Monster of Wasdale, her missive was delivered by a perspiring postman who had to ascend a flight of carpetless stairs to enter the editorial office of the *Gazette.*

The newspaper was read avidly (adverts an' all) by a populace who must be kept up to date with hatches, matches and despatches (births, marriages and deaths) and, under the Editorship of Reg Taffle, had names, names, names, which—said Reg—were the feature which sold a local newspaper. The *Gazette* was beginning to look like a telephone directory.

Reg did not so much sit as recline almost horizontally behind a roll-top task layered with paper, many of the sheets bearing tearings. Years of lolling had given him the knack of balancing his heavy wooden chair on two legs. His feet were on the topmost, ever-open drawer of a set of three. To achieve comfort, he unbuttoned the top three buttons of his trousers and all those of his waistcoat, which gave me a semi-peeled look. His trilby hat was, in the reclining act, worn at a rakish angle. So, when correcting galley proofs, this Editor-cum-contortionist peered through spectacles balanced on the end of his nose along his stomach to the proof, beyond which he could (if he moved the proof) see his (unfastened) shoes.

Reg had to adopt the normal sitting position to drink his tea, which he surreptitiously stirred his tea with a ballpoint pen. He hand-wrote his copy, denouncing the office typewriter as a

50

tripewriter. Said Reg: "Nothing but tripe comes out of it." The high-tech age had not arrived; the only mechanical item he possessed had only one moving part. This was the guillotine with which he carefully cut up A4 handouts from all manner of commercial concerns, using the backs as copy paper.

Reg shared the office with his staff, Tom Birl, a sub-editor of rather mournful disposition, as well he might with the normal type of news and gossip which passed through. The last time they had any excitement was when there was a report of Black Magic being practised at a remote churchyard. It was a hoax, of course. This Black Magic turned out to be a box of chocolates. More precise—a black box, with packing, the chocolates having been consumed by the local Rugby team, who set it all up for publicity.

They stared at the report of a Wasdale Monster. It was the Silly Season, when real news was scare. "I'll investiagte," said Reg.

Tom Birl had already given the story a catch-line—Wassie.

7: Media Interest

Reg Taffle, Editor of the *Cumberland Gazette,* forty years of age, divorced, and ready for a change from the musty air of the office, took the road to Wasdale Head. He had summoned a freelance photographer, Fred, who had been raised in the old school of plate cameras and flash-powder.

Fred, who was in dales parlance "nobbut t'size o' two pennorth o' copper", had progressed to flash-bulbs, and—being a man of frugal life-style—used part of a baked bean tin as a reflector. Now in his sunset years, Fred was working with a camera

51

which, he said, talked to itself. "It's forever clonking and buzzing."

The grandeur of Wasdale was slowly revealed to those hard-bitten newsmen. First there was what Reg called Alka Seltzer country because the many bends and dips churned up his stomach. Then the Screes, like a gigantic ski run (thought Reg, veteran journalist, to whom nothing was ordinary). Then the lake, with its cold blue look (a watery grave to Fred, who had photographed frogmen surfacing after examining the cold depths for the bodies of missing people).

A turn of the road brought the big fells into view—Gable, Kirk Fell, Yewbarrow, Scafell Pike (the last-named being, to Reg's journalistic mind, "the attic of Lakeland"). Reg had earned many a guinea in the old days writing about the local celebrity, Will Ritson, a droll man who told exaggerated tales, precourser of the modern tabloid journalist.

Reg's outlook on Lakeland was conditioned by his obsession for the good life, which he had not wholly found in Cumbria. He was a big-city man at heart. He was inclined to compare winter hills with iced wedding cakes and to describe a clear evening sky as being salmon-pink. The Lakeland becks ran gin-clear or, after storms, when the peat had been stirred up, resembled well-mashed (or broddled) tea.

Reg did not mind the countryside in small doses. But it tended to be dirty. And it was full of smelly animals. The Wasdale folk were a strange lot, with a language of their own—ax for ask, clobber for hit and fash for weary. He'd once queried an advert offering Fog to Let, which (he thought) must be the biggest con trick of all time. Excitedly, he made further inquiries. This was really Fog Grass, the second flush of growth in the meadows. Someone was being invited to put in some of their stock and eat it off.

They travelled in Fred's car, the type which Owd Jack referred to as "one of them pip-pipping sort". Fred was inclined to straighten out every road. He was impatient with other road-users, such as the flock of sheep they came across where the rolling road had regained its old status of a country lane.

Unhappily, the sheep were walking up the dale. Two men and three dogs were doing their best to control them. Fred, drawing alongside one of the perspiring men, said: "Whose the master of this flock?"

The farmer grunted before replying: "Yon little black-faced 'un at t'front!"

For Reg, the greys of everyday life developed into the reds and blues of ecstacy as he approached the bar of the *Woolsack* and saw a rich and varied assembly of drinks. The main snag to enjoyment this morning was work. There were times when even he, an Editor, must work.

He must chat with the tedious John Thwaite and this rural oddity, Mabel Seed, whom he had not previously met. With his journalistic instinct, he could picture her, though—a diminutive woman, with puckered up face, a nose which twitched, as though continually sniffing the air, steel-rimmed specs, head thatched with a bonnet, woolly clothes, thick black stockings and sensible shoes. Or even clogs, of the sort in which Beatrix Potter had clattered around the Lake District. Reg treated himself to the luxury of a smile. . . .

John Thwaite put on his general purpose smile and offered the Editor a whisky. After protesting it was too early in the day, and he had work to do, he downed it in a single eager gulp. Fred drank a pint of Hartley's ale so quickly it must have wetted only one side of this throat.

Reg, who prided himself on being a good judge of people, classified John Thwaite as Someone to Go Canny With. And he did not like the look of his lad, Jamie, who was the sort who'd let your car tyres down and then charge you for blowing 'em up.

John, with an eye to publicity, had planned an expedition to the fell where the hounds had been killed with the enthusiasm of a Mombasan arranging a big game hunt, though in Wasdale there was little call for pith helmets and khaki shorts.

The fellside was too steep and rocky for the all-terrain vehicle or even a Land Rover. Fred asked if there was a fell pony handy. It would look good on the photographs.

Mine-host obliged with a smile; he wished to advertise his pony trekking facilities, but was discouraged from putting a slogan on the saddle. Reg looked with distaste at the pony. He slipped Jamie 50p to look after it.

The *Woolsack* would be represented by Sean, the barman, who

53

(thought John) needed all the fresh air and exercise he could find. Sean was spending most of his life in the bar under strip-lighting and in an atmosphere which was usually about ten per cent cigarette and pipe smoke.

Mine-host was also glad to get the hyperactive Jamie from under his feet for a few hours. That lad was a pest, all the more so because his face had a bland appearance for most of the time. He might even look angelic, while his brain was clicking like an overworked computer, planning yet more mischief. Strangely, no one in his family had hitherto possessed a mop of red hair.

Reg, Editor of the *Cumberland Gazette*, "the newspaper you'll find at every fireside", as the masthead slogan had it, was about to about to encounter fell-country at close quarters for the first time. Sometimes when he was driving on the lowlands he ran into a belt of air polluted by slurry, which had lately been spread on the fields. It was as though an invisible hand was grasping his throat. What fetid odours lingered in the bracken he could not imagine. When pouring milk into his tea, he thought of supermarkets rather than the original production unit, a local shippon, with cattle having their teats fondled twice a day by cups of light alloy and rubber.

John Thwaite said: "The Monster was last seen by yon crag— the one with the rowan tree jutting out of it."

Reg scanned a hillside which looked as scarred and knobbly as a charlady's knees. "Oh, yes," he said, reassured that Jamie— the local lad—had been within earshot when the crag was identified. Reg's spectacles were beginning to steam up, a consequence of whisky and perspiration.

Jamie said: "When are you going to change your shoes, mister?"

Reg did not reply. Soon he had his suspicions confirmed. The terrain *was* dirty. He borrowed some cycle clips so that his tweedy trews would not drag in the mud.

The wretched fell pony was full of wind, expelling some with almost every footfall, with a sound like a ruptured bagpipe and—agony of agonies—the more he walked the more he sweat and the more attractive his forehead became to the wee critters of the hills, from bluebottles to clegs.

Jamie, lile lad though he was, was very well informed about

54

life, including the sex life of sheep-ticks. "If a lady tick doesn't have a good drink of your blood, it can't breed properly," said the lad.

Fred, the photographer, was not known as a prime burner-up of calories. The toughest work in his career as a photographer was to hire a step-ladder and carry it to where he could "shoot" over the heads of a crowd at a social gathering. He no longer borrowed a step-ladder. He still included the cost of hiring one as a legitimate expense.

In the lonnin (lane) the Monster Hunters had not over-exerted themselves. Now they were on the lower fell, flanked by a mini-jungle of bracken, the hazards to rural life were encountered. The little party was overtaken by a fell farmer and his dog, out leuking sheep, a Cumbrian form of stock-taking.

The farmer smiled that rural smile of amusement at the antics of off-comers who were slurring or stumbling. He sauntered by at an easy lope, not even having to drop a gear or two as the ground became brant, or steep. The boots on the farmer's feet looked as though they had been in a Round Britain Walk and were splayed out at the top. His dog, heading towards the pony, did an emergency stop when the farmer, without looking back, gave a three decibel whistle.

John Thwaite did not expect the Grand Monster Expedition, sponsored by the *Cumberland Gazette,* to be away for long. He didn't believe in Monsters. And no one was likely to be injured by an imaginery Monster. Mine-host had thought of crediting it with two heads, but decided that simplicity was best. A beast which resembled a herdwick tup was good enough. If you could inflate a herdwick till it was ten times bigger than normal, it would frighten the daylights out of anybody.

Fred, who led the way, camera at the ready, grimaced at the sight of a world scattered with sheep-droppings and the occasional steaming heap of dung from the ponies, doubtless the cousins of those carrying their gear, which seemed to infest the area. The fellside was intimidating, a sort of Stairway to Heaven. A beck gushed down a narrow, rocky, ankle-ricking course. The pony crossed without a glance. Jamie leapt from one smooth boulder to another. Reg, not noticing the difference in adhesion between bits which were wet and those that had dried out, skidded into the beck and winced as icy water seeped into a shoe.

The obstacle overcome, the Monster-seekers were on the intermediate land, where the ground was spongy, absorbing and holding moisture, sustaining a mass of sphagnum moss which, when disturbed, released from below a dozen odours never known in Arcady.

Then there was a thicket of gorse of the "oo, ouch" variety. A buzzard mewed as it spiralled against the blue vault of the sky. Reg, who felt it was laughing at them, decided that henceforth he would restrict his fellsides to views on picture postcards.

Reg called a halt. He was sweating profusely. Sweat stung his eyes and, with a salty taste, dribbled into his mouth. Another stretch of bracken lay ahead.

Jamie said: "If we don't hurry up, we won't be back for dinner." He was a growing lad, with a big appetite.

Fred suddenly groaned. He was not injured. Slapping his camera bag, he said: "I've left the film at the car. He went off like a spring rabbit before anyone could question it.

Another casualty came when the fell proper was reached. Here the ground was drier than it had been and bracken grew freely. Sean had a bad attack of barman's cramp and with profuse apologies, and just a little slurring of his words, said he would have to sit down and wait their return.

Which left Jamie in charge of affairs. This small, freckle-faced, red-haired lad had—thought Reg with a sudden flash of insight—an uncanny resemblance to the barman, who had been at the *Woolsack* for the requisite number of years. But perish the thought!

Jamie, as lively as a sheep-tick, grabbed the halter of the fell pony and led the way into another green jungle, where the bracken was shoulder high and any rocks were mossy and slippery—or slape, as Jamie said—and unyielding. Visibility was reduced to a few yards.

They stopped for a while as a passing cloud sprinkled the area with rain. Reg, being given the honour by Jamie to go first, discovered his principal job was to dislodge a billion droplets of water from the high bracken fronds. His clothes soon had affinities with well-used blotting paper.

The fell farmer and his dog, having found a better way up the fell, were now waving to them from the skyline. He shouldn't have gone to all the trouble of whistling as well. And why was he pointing towards them?

A rustling sound ahead alarmed Reg. For a few moments, it would have been possible to play a violin solo on his taut muscles. It turned out to be a herdwick yow—nowt special in this part of the world, but the daft animal, after sneezing at them, and having the whole fellside to go at, decided to take the trail they had blazed through the jungle, bowling Reg over and making the fell pony so nervous it reared, falling back on to its cup-like hoofs with an impact which seemed to shake the ground.

In the calm which followed the commotion, Jamie, mischievous as ever, brought into play what he called his Mark One Monster Detector—the largest stone he could lift. He lobbed it into the jungle of bracken.

What happened next was the subject of a few vivid impressions—nothing more. A large body, as big as a Shetland pony, thought Reg. when he was able to reflect on the incident, sprang into view. The main features were impressive. Horns like drop handlebars. Eyes that bored into him like gimlets. A big, greasy, gingerish body. A fetid smell. So much did Reg see before "it" struck him in the rear and knocked him full length, on his face.

Jamie, elated, confirmed Reg's impressions and added a few touches of his own. Steam was pouring out of its nostrils. The eyes were blood-red.

What the pony experienced was not known. It could not immediately be found. The load it had been carrying was picked up half a mile away.

To Sean O'Grady, sitting on a boulder, having a quiet smoke, the sudden appearance of the Monster drew from him the exclamation: "Jazus!" He hastily crossed himself and uttered a few Hail Marys, as the Monster broke cover, chased a few sheep, burst through a gate and scampered up the fell with the adroit footwork of a harried fox.

Friday's issue of the *Cumberland Gazette* alerted the district to the presence of something distinctly odd in Wasdale. The article was headed:

GAZETTE EDITOR ENCOUNTERS WASSIE

LAKELAND MONSTER TRACED
TO ITS LAIR

There were photographs, of course—Reg (head and shoulders), a brackenscape (with the Monster's size indicated by dotted lines). A beaming John Thwaite was portrayed at the bar of the *Woolsack*. A caption included the news (which was indeed news to John) that he was seriously considering a new name for his pub. It would be *The Monster*.

Reg began his article in a solemn way:

If anyone was to look for a monster in Wasdale they would doubtless buy a frogman's suit and descend into the depths of the deepest lake in England. Yet the monster which is terrorising this normally quiet dale is nothing like that at Loch Ness. Our Monster is terrestrial, big, gingery and likely to attack without provocation. It has already killed some hounds. A post office bus was so badly damaged it had to be taken out of service for several weeks for repairs. I came within stroking distance of it during an expedition mounted by the *Gazette*...

Wassie transformed Reg's life. When he had returned, exhausted and thirsty, from the wilds of Wasdale, mine host ushered him to the bathroom, told him to strip naked and pass his clothes out for attention while he washed the fellside muck from his person.

It was a big bath, a twenty-galloner. Mrs Thwaite had already drawn the water for him and placed a glass of whisky on a side table. Reg luxuriated in the soapy swell, sipping whisky and periodically poking his toes above water level to check on the transformation from pearl-white to glowing pink.

In one corner of the room were some spare clothes. Downstairs, Mabel Seed was waiting for him with another sheaf of copy, bound together in the top left-hand corner, as usual, by strands of knitting wool. Reg found that impressions gained from Miss Seed's work did not quite match up to reality.

58

Mabel Seed was not dishy, in the modern sense of female beauty—emaciation, to enhance the bone structure, with skin-tight clothes, lipstick and eye-shadow. She was—well—cosy. Livable with. She had intercepted him as he reeled towards the bar with a tongue so dry he might have struck a match against it. She had a motherly way with her and lots of sympathy for an Editor who had nearly died while on active service.

Mabel, somewhat middle-aged, tweedily clad, with men's shoes and stockings of coarse weave, was no beauty but was—well, restful. Her voice had a slight huskiness which made the hairs on Reg's nape stand on end, ready to be counted.

"My dear Miss Seed?"

She had flushed.

"I have been impressed over the years by your Wasdale news items."

The pink complexion reddened.

"I think you ought to come and join us in town. You could use your talents in so many ways."

Miss Seed said nothing. She just nodded.

A week after the publication of the Monster article, there she was, at her own desk in Reg's office, persevering with an electric typewriter and familiar with every feature of the tea-making facilities. She had a flat of her own in town. Reg was hoping that, ere long, he might once again launch himself on the swift tide of the sea of matrimony, as he might have put it, if he ever used a tit-bit of gossip about himself in one of his leading articles.

The jaunt organised for the *Cumberland Gazette* seemed to rile the Wasdale Monster. It was seen scattering sheep at the high grazings. It overturned a tractor, an old Grey Fergie, or so claimed the farmer, who trotted round to the insurance agent to inquire about compensation.

Daft Jimmy said he had heard Wassie calling at night. One time it was like "the braying of a sickly donkey" and another time, when there was a full moon, the cry was similar to that made by a fox "when it's caught its brush in a gate". No one took the last comparison seriously. When Jimmy found an audience, and began to tell them a tale, he tended to get carried away and to romance about it. And whoever had heard (much less seen) a fox opening and shutting a gate?

59

John Thwaite welcomed late season visitors to the Monster Bar at the *Woolsack*. He provided binoculars so that they might scan the fellsides, looking for Wassie. Timid farmers who were repairing drystone walls left the engines of their all-terrain vehicles running—just in case they needed to make a rapid escape. Children went uncomplainingly to bed when their mothers said that, if they were not good, t'Monster would get 'em.

A little more information about its appearance was forthcoming from fell-walkers who, when not looking at Mr Wainwright's book or their puffed-up feet, found a little time to admire the scenery. Each week-end, the fells were littered with walkers. From the descriptions, John Thwaite built up an Identi-kit picture—the sort he'd seen on television when the police wanted to catch a dangerous man they'd let out of prison by mistake.

The sketch showed an animal with a body rather like a mammoth (though not as big, of course). It was humpy, with a gingery-brown shaggy coat. The head was decked with some horns of awesome sight, not unlike those on one of Mr Attenborough's water buffalo's on t'telly.

The Monster was omniverous (it'd eat owt). A fearless rambler from Wigan said he had thrown it some sandwiches, then half a box of liquorice allsorts. A chap from Whitehaven who'd gone for a paddle in a mountain beck came back to find his boots had been half-eaten, though whatever had nibbled at 'em had not fancied the laces.

"Everyone's gone bluddy mad," said Isaac Tyson, yearning for a return to the peaceful old-time state of dale life. His daughter, Jane, going from farm to farm with her veterinary remedies, told him of the lass from London who was living in a cottage courtesy of Social Services. Now she was doing a bit of "moonlighting", producing Wassie in the form of a soft-toy, complete with squeaker, which operated when the woolly animal was pressed. Her soft toys, displayed at the village shop (price £3 each) were bought as souvenirs when she began to adorn each of them with a sticker—"A Present from Wasdale Head".

The doings at Wasdale Head, as reported in the *Cumberland Gazette*, set the Media Machine in motion.

First it was local commercial radio, sceptical but in need of some light-hearted material at a dark time of the year. Samantha Fullakin arrived with her new digital recorder. She captured on tape some of the more unusual farmyard sounds, like a coughing sheep, and then made a round of local farmers and, of course, visited John Thwaite who was by now so experienced in the technique of being interviewed he simply switched on to automatic pilot and delivered a string of cliches.

Listeners to *Daybreak*, the ten o'clock topical programme, after hearing a jingle about a new face-powder, had their blood chilled by the rasp of a bronchial sheep, followed by the sound of a Bronteish wind and then the brisk, no-nonsense tones of Samantha, a lass from Surrey who was feeling uneasy with her appointment on England's North West Frontier and could not understand even half of what the locals were saying.

She had a brief chat with a Friendly Neighbourhood Expert, who had first denounced the whole thing as bluddy daft but then, entering into the spirit of the thing, classified it as a throwback to some ancient Lakeland life form. A primeval sheep or goat. Or—his voice began to waver as he ran out of inspiration.

"Thank you," said Samantha. "We are going to organise a children's painting competition. Paint Wassie. I'll be giving details later . . ."

More coughing. More of the Bronte wind. Followed by an advertisement for constipation pills.

Then it was the turn of Summit Television, which filled in the odd half hour or so with local topics between adverts for soap powder and a torrent of media-mush beamed from London.

8: Wassie Strikes Again

Gerald Twitch-Bell, director of *Hangabout*, Summit TV's regular evening round-up of rape cases, celebrities with ghost-written books to publicise, and the latest football tittle-tattle, was keen to feature the Monster, alive or dead and preferably before whoever owned the critter had signed up with the opposition.

Gerald, a small man with a large ego, dressed like a fashion plate, had grown up in the fantasy world of television. Life had become one great Soap, broken down into sequences, each ending with a dramatic highlight. He saw people and places not as people and places but images, set in oblongs.

He bombarded the world with vivid images, gift-wrapped, and hoped there were enough people watching them to justify the advertiser's faith.

Television thrived on novelty. It must be larger than life. Everything had to be exaggerated. For "great", read huge. An advertiser of soap powder started his range with giant-size and went up the size and price range to a pack marked "mammoth".

Don't give anyone time to think, said Gerald Twitch-Bell. There must be no more than a second of silence at a time. The airwaves controlled by Summit Television sizzled with shrill voices and discordant strains.

A news presenter and camera crew were despatched to Wasdale. The young lady, Gertrude, was yet another bright young thing from the South, straight from Media College and given five days to read up about the Lake District before being set loose in it for programme material. It was the hope of Nigel Twitch-Bell that she could not only find and film the Monster but be seen patting it!

Mike, the cameraman, a veteran of ten thousand daft stories, had seen so much action around the world—including gorillas in the African rain forest—he was not likely to be moved to emotion by a hairy creature seen in westernmost Lakeland. In any case, Mike was rarely moved by anything these days. He was known to smile only on pay day.

No one on the studio floor knew the real name of the sound recordist. He hardly ever spoke and was nicknamed Titch. He let everybody else do the talking. He simply plugged his equipment into the camera and stood holding out a directional mike swaddled in a fluffy fabric which made it look like an unshaved sausage. Or even the offspring of a Hairy Monster.

Gertrude, an elegant lass who amused the dalesfolk because she "talked proper", heel-clicked her way into the *Woolsack*. There was one man—Henry Kilkoff—in the bar, and he was busy scribbling down some notes. Henry did not even look up as the film crew passed.

The sound recordist did not speak but he came to the rescue by imitating a trimline phone. *Brrr-brr, brrr-brrr, brr-brr.* John Thwaite scurried into view, looking bemused. He responded to the telephone, then suddenly remembered he did not have one of the trimline variety.

The city lass announced she was from Summit Television with the expectation that her hearers would either rush round to help or swoon with delight. Back in the studio there would have been a fanfare. John Thwaite (in expectation of entertaining some bigspenders) provided the welcome.

He showed her the newspaper artist's impression of Wassie. The picture was passed to Mike, the cameraman, whose face registered—nothing. He let the print fall to the ground. After that, nothing need be said about it.

Gertrude approached Henry. "Are you a native of these parts?"

"Shucks, no, honey," he replied, in his most exaggerated American speech. People now expected it of him and Henry, an amiable chap, was quick to oblige.

Gertrude looked at this long, languid, but remarkably goodlooking American with renewed interest. She could already see him taking part in the Television Spectacular. He would give the trans-Atlantic interest. Perhaps they could even arrange a hookup with an American channel.

63

Gertrude, in perfect control of her emotions, offered him a drink. They chatted. And Henry saw a way of making a mark on Jane Tyson. At least, if he was in the company of this strange young woman from television, she would not be able to ignore him.

Summit Television, at great expense, called their outside broadcast *Monster Spectacular*. They commissioned a special song—*Was-was-was-was-luvly-Wassie*—which was to be recorded by the Gayclops, the latest pop group sensation. When Nigel Twitch-Bell visited the valley by helicopter, overnight snow—just a scattering, above 1,000 ft—livened up the valley "televisionwise", as he was fond of saying. He had considered bringing up a snow machine to pep things up. Snow would also enable Tom Shunner, Lile Erne and "them Hoonds" to track the beast.

But first, they had to work the viewers up into the right mood. There'd be a Merrie Neet, presented live. "The way I see it," said Gerald, pacing up and down outside the *Woolsack*, occasionally stopping to look at the world through an oblong frame formed of thumbs and forefingers, "is we'll have a mixture of local and imported talent. We'll do a mock-up of a monster's head. Might sell the idea to Channel Twenty-Four, especially if we can find a few battered wives or kids in the dale."

"They're bluddy daft," said Isaac Tyson, when he heard of the plans. He sighed for the lost sanity of Wasdale. It was so peaceful in the old days.

The old men were all for daftness if it meant free ale—free in the sense it would be provided by Summit Television, who didn't mention they had come to an agreement with Ritson Breweries to sponsor it, providing their name was well-displayed.

Isaac Tyson declined to take part. Most of the other dalesfolk thought of it as a way of shortening the long, cold winter. At an introductory meeting, a special barrel of ale was on tap. Dales farmers with a partially for summat stronger than lemonade picked up delicate vibrations and subtle chemical changes in the Wasdale air which proclaimed: free ale. A frenzy of activity followed. Men changed into their better clothes and decent footwear. Each followed their inclinations and were led unerringly to the bar of the *Woolsack*.

A new hunting song had been provided by the public relations department of the brewery:

Come gather together, ye Men of the Dale
—tally-ho, tally-ho;
And follow the Hounds (not dogs) to Good Ale
—tally-ho;
We'll follow Tom Shunner, from *t'Woolsack* to Gable
And sup Ritson Drinks as well as we're able
—tally-ho, tally-ho, tally-ho.

It was a reet good do. Nobody could remember when more ale were supped and more ale spilt on t'bar floor. There was incessant talk about Wassie. He was no longer feared, despite the mounting list of damage, such as dinged cars, gapped walls, even broken windows.

Lakeland insurers who kept graphs showing the financial undulations of their strange and unpredictable business suddenly found they had a crisis on their hands. The normal wavering line was now showing the makings of a majestic peak, with no plateau in prospect. It looked as though they were in the process of refurbishing the entire dale. From Dalehead to Dalefoot, the property had never looked neater.

Suspicions were aroused when Wassie stood accused of lighting a fire in somebody's bedroom.

Henry Kilkoff, in his little cottage, with slates replaced and unnecessary gaps plugged, settled into the routine of filing all the information he was collecting about Wasdale Past. He tended to rise early, scribble for an hour or so then go for a walk, through the birch wood to the open fell, and trudging on to Raven Pike, with the ravens putting on an air display for him, circling, hanging on the wind with undercarriages lowered to maintain their equilibrium or flipping upside down, then back again, their coarse voices coming as near as ravens could manage to cries of joy.

Then it was back to his research. Of course, Henry came across lots of references in local books to Will Ritson, dalesman extraordinary, and teller of tall tales, including one of a giant turnip—so big they excavated bits from it and these fed them for a year, the shell of the turnip being used as a shed in which the

Ritsons kept a plough and an old cart. He liked Jos Naylor's creation, which was a herdaroo, being a cross between a herd-wick sheep and a kangaroo. By carrying its lambs in a pouch it kept them safe from marauding foxes.

Owd Jack let him borrow a Flock Book of the Herdwick Sheep Breeders' Association. Henry read that a typical sheep had a strong coat of flowing wool. The belly must be covered. "A thin or fine coat would be useless to withstand the storms of hail and snow in winter. The top of the head should be carried high, broad across the forehead, deep on the jaw, wide at the nostrils, arched nose and with a bold prominent, well-developed eye." The man who wrote this was something of a poet!

At other times, Henry slipped his tape-recorder and notebook into his old rucksack and headed for the *Woolsack,* the source of endless local tales from men whose tongues were loosened by ale. Especially Simeon Humma, who had an individualistic way of imparting information.

Henry asked him about his sheep, to be told: "When you've been fetched up wi' herdwicks, it's a way of life. A herdwick's good at standing t'weather i' these parts. . . A sheep's not poorly for long; it either gits better or dies off. . .''

Henry asked about sheepdogs, to be told: "You have to have a pup or two coming on. You nivver know when an old dog'll drop out of a crag or just tottle off on you or git run over down t'road. . .There's a pup in t'house just now. It's mother didn't want it, so we treat it like a baby. It sleeps beside our bed and squeaks every four hours for a feed. . .''

And there were some comments about landscape and townsfolk who mess it up: "They usually blame t'sheep but we know what's done most o' t'damage. It's t'Commando sole. Some of the fells which had a few sheep tracks are now mucked up. They're in a reight scrow." Simeon, asked to explain "scrow" said: "A mess." Henry wrote down beside scrow —untidy!

By the third pint, Simeon was in a reminiscent mood. He'd heard of the days when home-brewed beer was made from dandelions and nettles. Before the winter set in, hams of mutton were smoked in a big chimney over peat fuel. "Aye, most o' what they ate lived in t'dale." Cows gave milk, which was

66

separated, the cream used for making butter, some of it used for mixing with tar to salve sheep in November. A lot of summer butter was salted down in special tubs and used in winter.

Back in the hut, Henry wrote till his eyes prickled and his fingers ached. One evening, as he prepared for his fact-gathering jaunt, he thought he heard the sound of a passing tractor but dismissed the idea, for it was long after dark. The only tractor hereabouts belonged to Owd Jack. Come to think of it—Jack had a reckless disregard of the law and was known to visit the pub on a tractor which had no lights and, if truth be known, an out-of-date insurance.

The doctor told Jack that if he didn't renew it, he'd report him. Then he'd lose his licence. "You'd hev a job on," said Owd Jack, "cos I haven't got one."

Henry left the cottage. It was beginning to snow—not the sloppy stuff, carried by a westerly wind, but big flakes, from a cloud which had slowly drawn a curtain across the moon. The snow, coming from the north-east, was sticking.

As Henry walked down the track to the road, he detected the lingering traces of diesel fuel. Then thoughts of the evening's merriment took over. His long legs soon covered the one and a-half miles to the *Woolsack*.

It was another "lang neet". Throats dried out through constant chatter and were kept lubricated by ale and whisky. Sean O'Grady, the barman, had extra help. The ale flowed like peat-watter in a beck after a storm.

At an hour when god-fearing folk had been in bed for ages, Sean (befuddled with drink) opened the door to the cellar, to attend to the barrels. He carried an electric torch, the day-lighting strip in the cellar having been on the blink. Sean slurred his feet as he made a slow descent of the stone steps.

Sean smelt ale, of course. There was also a musky, armpit sort of smell. The torchlight cut cleanly through the air, revealing the arching of the roof, with its little stalactites, formed at the cracks over many years.

Some of the barrels had been moved. A bottle or two had fallen and shattered on the stone flags. With a prickle of fear crossing his head, questing for his spine, Sean shone the torch around the cellar.

And there was the Devil himself, come to claim him.

The light brought a responsive ruby-red gleam from eyes which looked as big as saucers. The old stories were right. The Devil had horns. In a moment, Sean's recent life flashed before him. He thought of his iniquities—double marks on the slate in the bar and, may god help him, much watering of the ale.

"Jazus!" exclaimed Sean, as he heard a scraping of horn against slate and just before something as rough as sandpaper blundered past him. He fainted.

Amos and others brought the limp form of Sean O'Casey into the light. Each man commented on the dank smell in the cellar.

Henry, rushing outside, saw marks in the snow. The marks indicated some large and heavy creature had blundered away, on a far-from-straight course. And he laughed. Whatever it was had a skin full of strong drink.

Mine-host said: "Who put the bluddy Monster down there?"

9: A Gey Lang Winter

For several months, the Monster slipped from reality into folklore. In November, sex reared its ugly head in Wasdale as another tupping time arrived. The dale farmers smeared the underparts of their tups with a dye which would be transferred during copulation to the rumps of the yows. So they kept check on the progress of the mating season and could determine when the lile lambs would begin to arrive.

The X-certificate stuff was also evident in a number of local bedrooms. With the dark nights at hand, some of the dale farmers grew restive. Their ladies became pregnant. As one man said to a friend at t'auction mart: "Thoo can't spend all thi spare time watching telly."

Henry's ambitions to get to see more of Jane took a turn for the worst when he was found in the arms of another woman. It was on yet another social occasion, this time the annual dance of the Young Farmers' Club, notable for the venue (an annexe of the hotel) and the decor, which traditionally consisted of bales of hay and streamers of toilet paper of various hues. Basic catering included scones brought around in wicker baskets and the tea in buckets, to be transferred to cups held by the thirsty dancers via an enamel jug.

Henry arrived early and stood with restless eyes, questing for Jane. Suppertime came. A door was swung open. Members of the committee appeared, carrying trestle tables, loaded with scones. Others, with tea duty, began the ritual round with a bucket.

Simeon said to Henry: "Get up, Yank, and shake thee supper down." He did, in a progressive dance, after which he stood around, aimlessly, awkwardly, until the door opened and into the room stepped a gorgeous creature, a blonde clad in a red dress. The lower jaws of those nearest the door drooped with astonishment. One young farmer pawed the ground with his shoes, pretending to be an eager tup.

Simon was flabbergasted. Turning to his neighbour, he said: "Why didn't they make lasses like that when I was a lad?"

His neighbour happened to be Henry, whose face lit up, not because of the Young Lady in Red but because Jane had now appeared. With her was Tony. Henry advanced towards her, only to be intercepted by the stranger. Only it wasn't a stranger. They knew each other of old. The girl with the red dress threw her arms around his neck and gave him a kiss which was as noisy as it was succulent.

"By heck," said Simeon, "it were just like a cow takkin' its foot out of a swamp."

Henry did not resist. They became leg-locked, as Simeon put it. Momentarily, Jane was forgotten. Henry glanced in her direction. She looked flustered and, to Tony's surprise, was making a special fuss of him, knowing the eyes of the room were upon her. Then they were gone. Henry and the young lady disentangled themselves but continued to hold—indeed, squeeze—each other. She ruffled his hair. They jabbered at each other. And then they were gone, with some of the assembly pinching themselves, for confirmation that they had not been in a dream sequence.

Rumour had it that Henry and his young lady spent the night together in Henry's little cottage and, early next morning, he arranged for a taxi to take her to the station. For once, rumour was correct.

There had been a rush when Henry asked if any of the young farmers would drive them to the cottage. The successful lad was Thomas, Isaac Tyson's brother's lad, who had never been in such close proximity to a girl who was as vivacious and sweet-smelling and excitingly dressed as this young lady.

On his return to the dance hall, he related what had happened to a muster of dancers. He confirmed that she was American. She had a drawly voice, like Henry's, but she wasn't chewing her cud. It was Thomas's little joke about chewing gum.

"Aye," said the lad, "there were three of us on t'front seat of t'Land Rover. Yon lass couldn't keep her hands off him. They chattered away, ten to a dozen. While Henry went to switch t'light on, she gave me a smacking kiss as well. I don't think I'll wash that part of mi face again.

"The hussy," said Simeon, enviously.

"They went in. And it wasn't long afore there was just a bedroom light burning. By gum, but Henry's a fast worker."

The Wasdale Monster kept out of sight but left its trade-mark (as Simeon put it) everywhere. It had developed the knack of lifting gates off hinges, which was a variation on the theme of charging them. The beast operated close in to the village, where it breached the defences of the gardens. Footloose herdwicks extended their menu to include wall-flowers.

Fred Hagg, taking a far-from-straight course home after a night at the *Woolsack,* had to resort to blundering. The village lantern (which t'owd chaps called the moon) had gone behind a cloud. Fred instinctively reached out for his garden gate. He was not too worried when he did not find it immediately, for on several occasions, in similar conditions, his outstretched arm had found the space between bars. His nose had been the first to come in contact with the woodwork.

This night, however, he missed touching the gate three times and advanced to find himself ankle deep in bits of wood, the remains of his gate. A trail of enormous hoof-prints across the garden marked the Monster's escape route.

Next morning, one of the shattered gate posts was found to have trapped a piece of gingerish wool.

Henry telephoned Jane but each time he heard her reply there was an almost immediate click as the telephone was disconnected. He met Isaac. "What's ta done to t'lass?" he said. "I've never known her so moody. Now she's talking about wedding Tony. That'll never do."

Christmas came and went with the usual Lakeland routine of hard work and, for an hour at the kirk, the annual carol service, with the kids dressed up as Biblical characters. There was usually a schoolyard fight over who was going to play Joseph.

Summit Television included Wasdale in its *Hymns My Old Mother Used to Sing* series, by Mona Littlehorn, wearing her sanctimonious expression. She was said to be a great personality. Amos said: "Nivver heard on her!"

For the recording, every pew was creaking with the weight of worshippers. Henry contrived to sit beside Jane, to her annoyance. They had not met each other since the night of the dance. He did not want the service to end. She wanted to move. But there was no other seat for her to occupy.

Henry leaned towards her. "Say.."

Jane found herself stiffening. The blood seemed to drain from her head.

"Say. . . ."

She squirmed in her embarrassment.

"Jane. . .what did you think of Polly?"

He was actually gloating.

"She dropped off on her way back to the States."

This was too much.

"One day I'd like you to meet her. She's my favourite sister."

Jane, numb with shock and remorse, found Henry's right hand and clasped it. She waited for her blood circulation to resume.

"Say. . .you were jealous."

"With a dress as red as that, who could blame me?"

In the lile kirk, on Christmas Eve, Henry and Jane were friends again. For once, Jane had time to get ready for an appointment. She smelt of scent rather than farm-muck. She had a

71

pert nose. And—yes—her eyes *were* hazel.

To Jane, Henry's droll name and languid manner seemed, now that the identity of the glamorous blonde had been revealed, to conceal a thoroughly nice and dependable person. He was tall. So what? He had a slightly foisty, cottage-in-the-backwoods smell. Which was not surprising. He chose to live at the back-o'-beyond. And his eyes were blue.

> *O little town of Bethlehem,*
> *How still we see thee lie!*
> *Above thy deep and dreamless sleep*
> *The silent stars go by . . .*

Jane gave a soft chuckle—and Mona Littlehorn broke the first rule of television and gasped—as Minnie, presiding at the harmonium, over-awed by the bright lights and television cameras, became flustered and struck a few wrong notes. The producer broke the Christmas spell by insisting the verse should be sung once again.

> *. . . Yet in thy dark street shineth*
> *The everlasting light;*
> *The hopes and fears of all the years*
> *Are met in thee tonight.*

They sat down and Henry's right hand once again quested for Jane's. It was a little drama enacted out of sight of the television cameras and the media folk in the control van, which was parked in the lane.

Jane's part in the Christmas programme ended, and another production problem occurred, during the singing of *Silent Night* when her mobile phone began to ring. As she rose, on the blind side of Tony, she flashed Henry a smile which dazzled him. Henry now made the mistake of singing *Silent Night* with too much gusto.

He stood among homely folk, with a wash of words, and a distinctive Lakeland inflection, and began to understand the dalesfolk, with their thousand year old tradition, alongside which the Media intrusion seemed tawdry.

They sang a hymn composed in dialect, the old speech of Cumbria, though it had been "wattered doon" a bit for this television

72

occasion. It went to *Nativity,* yan of t'auld tunes:

Brought up wid t'sound o' becks and gills
And t'sough-en wind in t'dark,
With thunder rolling round brant hills;
Blithe songs of many a lark.

Three boys had been bribed to play the t'Wise Men in the nativity play. Henry chuckled as one of the lads invested some familiar words with a Cumbrian flavour: "Whear is 'e that's born t'King of t'Jews. We've sin his star in t'east and we've come to worship 'im." Girls fluttered about as angels with white nightdresses and paper-mache wings.

The Benediction was pronounced. The last hymn was sung. Summit Television signed off. The big arc lights—and the Christmas magic—were switched off.

In a local barn, strewn with straw, Jane—one arm almost up to the armpit in the backside of a dairy cow—struggled to correct the position of a calf in the womb. The tough farmer watched this slip of a girl. She spurned help. She paused for a minute or two to muster more energy.

She pulled hard. Suddenly, the calf was born—a gangly, limp, sloppy form, twitching on its bed of straw. The cow called to the calf—a low, gentle sound—and then turned and began to lick the calf clean.

The farmer looked at his watch. It was past midnight. He turned to Jane and said: "Merry Christmas, lass."

Henry, whose bathroom on warm days had been the nearest beck, was in the habit of calling on Owd Jack on a winter evening for a bath. As the departing sun reddened the Screes and the air chilled, he slipped gratefully into an easy chair beside Jack's huge fire of coal and wood, with one or two turves of peat to flavour the place.

The fire was so hot that when, with Jack's approval, he turned on the taps in the bathroom prior to having his weekly once-over (as Jack called it), the water pipes vibrated and steam rolled around the room and down the chilly upstairs passage of the farm like fog on the Newfoundland Banks.

Then it was back to the fire. Henry would open a bottle of whisky he had brought. Owd Jack, with traditional Lakeland

73

hospitality, chucked the cork at the back of the fire and gave his gummy smile as he said: "We won't need that again."

Said Jack, one night: "Isn't it time thoo settled doon and git wed?"

Henry did not reply. He projected on to the wide screen of his mind a picture of Jane Tyson, as he had last seen her, singing her heart out in the cosy, homely village church.

Jack laughed. "I yance knew a chap who courted a lass for fourteen years. She said: 'Isn't it time we got wed?' And he answered: 'Aye, lass—but who'd have us'?"

In early January, the howling of vixen foxes was followed by the answering yaps of love-lorn males. It was courting time for foxes. Unshaven farmers and bearded ramblers strode across the fells.

It seemed as though the insurance companies had the Monster in check—for a while.

Isaac Tyson said: "I reckon your Monster's hibernated."

"Nay," said Jonty Gill, his postmanly demeanor now fully restored, "it'll be ligging dead in one of t'gills, being picked ower by crows."

The laggard spring arrived. Moderating conditions were wafted up the dale from the sea and then fought their way to the tops, melting the snow and the ice which had crusted the ancient joints of the fells. Yet there were days when silvery hailstones bombarded the dale.

Daffodils appeared in farm gardens. The weather became dry if chilly. Farmers began to whistle again. The first touroids appeared, as regular in their timing as the cuckoo which called from the old sycamore at the end of a farmstead.

Owd Jack said to Henry: "There's summat special happening tomorn. Leave it clear."

Henry obeyed.

At first light, he saw Jane's car parked beside the lane leading to Jack's farm.

Said Jack: "I was bahn to show you a raven's nest. But when I woke up this morn, I hedn't much wind. (He wheezed and rubbed his chest). I've pointed it oot to t'lass. She'll take you." He gave Henry a wink.

Henry and Jane spent a day in Jack's little kingdom—the corrie

74

and adjacent fellsides. New bracken was sprouting. It had just reached the stage at which each sappy stem had a head on it like a bishop's crozier.

Wheatears were back from Africa. They heard their hard calls—*chack, chack*. Also to be heard was the male's song—a strange warbling refrain, at times sweet, at other times with an asthmatic wheezing. Rather like Owd Jack.

Jane, looking happy now she was off duty and stress-free, went up the brant fell like a goat. Henry lumbered behind. He stopped to admire the view. And had one or two surreptitious glances in the direction of Jane.

The breeze drew a comb through the coarse grasses and rush-bobs. The dalehead, with its amazingly flat fields, had upon it the first flush of green. They faintly heard the clatter of a bucket and some coarse words, rising from where Jack was attending to his stock.

Said Jane: "Jack's been saying some nice things about you."

They were sitting—or trying to sit—on a grassy slope which was as steep as a house side.

Jane slithered. Henry held her and made a clumsy attempt to kiss her. She stiffened in his arms. He released her immediately.

She was still for a moment, looking fixedly into the dale. She looked incredibly slight and young, with her thatching of dark hair. Jane, the tough one—she who, as a vet, operated almost at the limits of her strength as she helped to bring calves into the world; who thought nothing of plunging an arm deep into a cow to correct the position of a breached calf—was actually blushing.

What could she make of this gangling American who was a stranger in Wasdale and yet had such an affinity with it? Who had little of the Lakeland reserve and responded to impulse?

Said Jane: "Try again." Their lips met and for a minute or two might have been moulded to each other.

Jane sprinted ahead. Henry, woefully ill-shod, slipped and slithered. She helped him up one of the steeper bits. The hand-clasp was firm.

Eventually they stood at the rim of the corrie, with the male raven giving its kronking call as it glided through the air, periodically flicking on to its back in its agitation, then flicking back again, when the glossy black plumage acquired silvery highlights from the bright sun. The raven's legs dangled to help it maintain balance as it hovered in the updraught from the corrie. Then the bird landed, peevishly pulling up tufts of grass.

Said Jane: "It's telling us to clear off."

Henry flopped. His chest rose and fell like a blacksmith's bellows.

Jane laughed. "It's true what they say about Americans..."

"Which is?"

"They're wealthy—but soft. They ride about too much. The next generation will be born on casters."

Henry did not disagree. He was just thankful to have Jane's company.

She led him along the rim of the corrie, periodically stopping to look down, the draught blowing her hair until at times it was standing on end pressing her clothes against her so that the firmness of her young body was revealed in contoured beauty.

"Here's the nest."

Now there were two ravens in the air. Their calls varied from a deep *prruuk* to clucking notes. They drifted away, as though anxious not to draw any further attention to their nest.

Janet stood at the rim of the corrie, the face bright. Henry crawled to the edge, peered over it, felt the blast of air pushing his spectacles against his face. His cap flew off and was bowled along like a windblown leaf.

Below them, on a rock ledge, was a nest made of large twigs. Within the nest reposed an amorphous mass of young ravens, with four heads, sporting powerful beaks and bright eyes, sticking from it.

Henry watched, stiff with fear, as Jane slipped over the edge, clutched a small rowan tree growing from a crack, and went down a grassy slope to the ledge, using her rump as a sledge. She drew from the nest one of the young ravens and clambered back. For the last steep pitch, she needed help from Henry, who gratefully slipped an arm round her slender waist.

The nestling she had brought with her would not have won a beauty competition. It was dull and dishevelled, with feathers developing behind quills. They collectively reminded Henry of a woman wearing curlers. One of the bird's eyes was opaque. Lodging beside it was a hair. Jane carefully withdrew the hair.

76

She sat, nursing the bird, watching as the brightness returned to its eye. Then she returned the nestling to the company of its brothers and sisters.

Henry said: "How old are you?"

"Twenty-six."

"I'm thirty-seven."

"An old man."

Jane, laughing, went off down the hill, leaving Henry to stumble along behind her. By the time he arrived at the farm, she had driven off.

Owd Jack said: "I hope thoo med thi best of things."

Henry replied, without too much conviction: "I sure did."

It was lambing time. Herdwick yows brought down from the fellsides to the big flat fields near the farms began to part with their lile black lambs. Hill sheep were tough. They did not usually need the services of a midwife, yet when complications arose, and the farmer wanted help, Jane's four-wheel drive vehicle scurried about the dale.

Most often, the farmer dealt with sheep matters themselves. Henry called to see Isaac (disappointed when he found Jane was not at home) and he went with the farmer on a round of the crofts. The farmer carried his crook and had one of his dogs at foot. Having false teeth, he could not whistle as he used to do and the commands to the dogs were shouted.

The soprano calls of new lambs mingled with the contralto voices of the ewes. Henry watched a new-born lamb being coaxed on to its stilt-like legs by its parent.

"A Swaledale's a better mother," said Isaac. "The herdwick tends to be a bit too proud. It backs off." The lamb was soon questing for the teats. Its success was measured by the brisk wagging of the long tail which would soon be reduced in length, the tip wasted away as a small rubber ring placed by Isaac had its effect.

The ewe turned to sniff at the lamb, to ensure it was her own. Otherwise, she would have butted it away. The lamb looked pathetically small against the fleecy bulk of the ewe. Isaac, using his shepherd's crook of sheep horn with a hazel shaft drew the lamb to him and innoculated it.

He said, grimly: "Before we turned sheep into pin cushions,

77

my old dad might wheel a barrow full of dead lambs out of the fields. It was terrible.''

Isaac laughed. Then explained how an orphan lamb, brought up as a pet, thrived mightily. It could also be a bit of a nuisance, entering the house. ''Jane had a pet lamb. One day we were dipping sheep. We picked up the lamb and threw it into the dip with the rest. Then we regretted it.'' He laughed again. ''Yon lamb ran straight into t'house and shook itself before t'fire.''

A day that began cold and dry, which suited the lambing sheep, ended with snow flurries from the north-east. Soon the tops of the fells were powdered white. Snowflakes danced in the gap between Gable and Scafell Pike, from which came the worst of the weather.

Isaac talked about a lazy wind, adding: ''It's too lazy to go round and tries to cut straight through you.''

They returned to the kitchen for pint pots of tea, ''hot as hell, black as t'fireback''. Jane's mother had some fresh scones, laced with rum butter.

Henry and Isaac walked round the fields yet again. Most of the sheep were in the lee of the walls where stones intercepted the snowflakes but permitted the wind to blow through, keeping the sheep dry.

They found a lile lamb which had an eye pecked out by a carrion crow. There had been twin lambs. The other was already sucking.

''I don't like a lot o' twins,'' said Isaac. ''Mother hasn't enough milk and time to rear two. This 'un would be attacked by a crow as t'ewe struggled to give birth to the other.''

Henry picked up the lamb. It hung limply from his hand. He listened to its pathetic cries and to the deeper voice of the ewe which followed him, the other lamb trotting at foot in short, sharp bursts of energy.

The lamb was fearfully maimed, and it continued to hang from his hand with the limpness of old sacking. But Henry felt its heart beating strongly. It would cling on to life.

In the kitchen, which was stripped for action, the horse-hair sofa was covered with rugs so that one of the men might cat-nap during the night. Henry sneaked a glimpse of a photograph of the newly-graduated Jane, looking pert and pretty.

Tony was attending to a chilled orphan lamb. Henry had to admit that Tony was a dab hand with farm stock.

He watched, astonished, as Tony plunged a red-hot poker into a can of milk, then poured the warm milk into a bottle to feed the lamb. It had to be coaxed, then sucked impatiently. And when it was done, the lamb was slipped into the side oven for a few minutes to complete its recuperation.

Said Isaac, grimly: "This lamb will be cooked three times. Yance lightly, in t'oven. Yance on t'hill this summer. And yance this back-end, when it's young mutton."

Henry shuddered at the thought.

Isaac said: "When we take that lamb out, we'll have to find a sheep to take it over."

In the big barn, which was festooned with ancient cobwebs and was now almost empty of hay, pens had been set up to create a hospital for sheep and chilled or ailing lambs. Henry watched enthralled as a dead lamb was skinned, the skin slipped over the spare lamb and lowered into a lile pen, hoping that the lingering smell of the dead lamb whose fleece was now being worn like a jacket would persuade the sheep to accept another.

Henry often saw the ravens, which had synchronised the appearance of their young with the abundance of food, from a ewe's afterbirth to the yow itself. A number of sheep succumbed to one of a dozen quaintly-named sheep diseases. He was astonished how many skeletons of sheep he found in cracks, crannies and gills. A gill had become a veritable Valley of the Dry Bones.

One of Jack's lambs was found drowned in the beck. The mother ewe was on her back, 'rigged'. Jack, knowing she'd been there for some hours, was careful how he turned her, not wishing to cause injury. And he held her up for a while until the blood was again circulating normally and she was steady on her legs.

Several lambs were taken by a fox which had not been hungry. It had slain them in a frenzy and left them littered across the field.

On one of his walks, Henry found a cragfast sheep. The herdwick had been tempted from one ledge to another by the first flush of new growth and was now on a yard wide ledge with an awesome drop beneath it. Henry volunteered to help, but Jack

79

mustered one or two members of the local rescue team.

A couple of ropes were secured to thorn trees on the fell. One rope, tied using a bowline, went round the rescuer and the other was a lifeline. He descended, brushing the mossy cliff, to where the sheep stood.

"Chuck a few stones over t'side so t'sheep will hear 'em and know there's a big drop. I don't want it killed."

Henry chucked some stones, as requested. The herdwick did not want to be caught but eventually the rescuer had it in a sort of bear-hug. The greasy body and its fetid tang nauseated him. He got a spare rope tied round it and, with a few mighty heaves, the sheep was raised, followed by a grinning man.

Owd Jack's best land was near Henry's cottage. The lanky American followed him around the fields, noting how he used his lambing-crook to gather up sheep in difficulties, or lambs he wished to examine. The crook shot out with the speed of an adder's tongue, arresting an animal which the old man soon gathered up.

Said Jack: "Things are going too well. And I haven't seen a fox yet."

He spoke too soon. That very night, half a dozen of his lambs were worried by a fox which took a bite out of one of them and played with the others just for fun. One lamb was only slightly injured.

"Noo's your chance."

Henry raised his eyebrows.

"Thoo knaws nowt about sheep farming. So tak this lamb down to Jane's surgery and tell her you found it. T'owd yows deeard so she won't miss it. Then bring it back to me and if I can't mother it on, I'll just have to raise it as a pet."

Henry plodded to the village in the rain. Hours of teeming, tippling precipitation brought the becks out in flood and filled the cellar of the *Woolsack,* also the wellies of anyone who had forgotten to take them indoors the previous evening.

Said Jane: "This is one of Jack's lambs. Is he match-making again?"

"Again?"

"He's a crusty old bachelor himself. But he likes to see other's wed."

80

Said Henry, daringly: "He's got plans for us."

"Of course."

"I'd like to meet you. Go out for an evening. A meal, perhaps?"

"That's not the dale way. I'll be going to the dance on Friday evening."

Henry did not pursue his inquiries. He left the surgery with a light tread. Jane called after him: "Haven't you forgotten something?"

He flushed—and went back for the lamb.

The dance, one of the run-of-the-mill-variety, took place in the Institute which was, by intent, just a stone's throw—or a drunkard's lurch—from the *Woolsack*. The name Institute sounds posh, but this was an old Army hut (first world war vintage) which during its military service held a stove, table, two forms and walls lined with bunks.

The Wasdale men had bought it cheap. Isaac Tyson's father moved it, in pieces, from Ravenglass station. It was left in a big heap for the whole of one winter—a cold winter, when bits of it were taken and burnt to warm the rooms at local homes.

Come springtime, and the men erected what was left and raised money to complete the hut, making a fairly good job of it. The main trouble was that it had no proper foundations. If there were some lively dances, the whole structure tended to move a few yards.

The dance was advertised for 7-30. At that time only two things were moving—the caretaker and a bottle of whisky. Henry arrived at 8-0, expecting the dance to have reached a lively stage. A few lights were burning and the womenfolk were gossiping as they buttered bread for the sandwiches. One or two morose dancers were standing near the heating unit—an old-fashioned, sit-up and beg iron stove which some genius with combustibles had coaxed into a brilliant white heat.

"Don't go too near yon stove," said the doorkeeper to Henry, "or you'll be sucked into it."

At 8-30, two men entered the room with iron bars, which were slipped through either side of the stove. A tap with a hammer disconnected the pipe above it and the stove was carried out of the hut and left in a corner of the car park.

81

At 8-45 the band arrived—the *Twa Craws*, from Eskdale. A buxom lass from a lowland farm who seemed to fancy Henry explained the band's name for his benefit. It was Twa (two) Craws (crows). Henry, loosening up, chuckled. "It sure sounded odd—like a suburb of Peking!"

The buxom lass screwed up her face quizzically.

The oldest "craw" began playing a lively Cumberland tune, and the younger "craw", his son, was soon raining blows on the drums. Henry looked around. There were maybe a dozen couples on their feet, following the owd-time dancing ritual like automata. They'd plainly been dancing for most of their lives.

He crossed to the *Woolsack* and met some of the young farmers of the dale. It was a whisky round, followed by a gin round, followed by ale just in case there were some corners of the digestive system which remained untouched by alcohol. The buxom lass joined in and was still drinking when the others were wondering why the room was spinning.

They all returned to the dance. It was frosty outdoors and, by now, stiflingly hot in the hall. Henry's world was about to fall apart. As he stared through eyes which seemed to have been covered with frosted glass, he was vaguely aware of a buxom farm lass at his side. She pulled him on to the floor for a dance. And spun him round. It was a progressive dance. He was passed on to another, then another, then—Henry fell in a crumpled heap, not far from the band. One of his new friends revived him.

The *Twa Craws* almost awakened the dead with their strident music. The dancers ebbed and flowed like a sharp tide. Forward, backward, sideways, twirl. Repeated. For a few seconds, as one dancer succeeded another, he revelled in the touch of Jane's warm, muscular body under a floral dress. Then she was gone, into the swirling mass, under the flashing lights, accompanied by Big Craw's surge of raucous music, with Little Crow continuing to beat out the rhythm on the drums.

Henry sat out the next dance. It was The Lancers, a sedate dance given a wild rendering by the younger end, who were mainly in the Young Farmers' Club, with plenty of surplus energy. As they stepped out, the hall danced with them. As they swung their partners—wildly, with feet leaving the ground—the hall swayed. One luckless lass, who slipped from her partner's grasp, slithered half way down the hall and crashed into a bevy of spectators.

When Tony was dragged on to the floor by one of his old flames, Henry had the next dance with Jane. The tune was *Loch Lomond*, one of his favourites. Och, aye. Life was good. A romantic atmosphere was induced when a big dazzling globe began to spin and someone put a beam of light on it. The walls were filled with a peacock's tail of silvery forms.

He danced Jane out of the hall and walked her to her car. It seemed natural for them to clamber into it and for Jane to drive him to her home. They never stopped for an instant to think how Tony might get back.

The ticking of a grandfather clock in the living room and the glow of embers from a fire which had been half coal, half peat, give it a warm and friendly appearance. Jane prepared mugs of tea. They sat in the fireside glow, talking, enjoying their nearness to each other, until a creaking from above signified that Isaac Tyson was astir. Henry was pushed into a space under the stairs. The creaking boards immediately above his head indicated the progress of Isaac's be-slippered feet.

"Nah then, lass, are you by yourself?"

"Aye."

"Make sure the door's locked and the fireguard's in place before you come up to bed."

"Aye."

Henry, peeping round a corner, saw a Dickensian apparition. Jane's father wore a flannel nightgown. He carried a candle in a large holder.

When he had returned slowly up the stairs, there was just time for a hug and a kiss. Jane let Henry out of the house. He walked joyfully through the frost-stiffened night. He did not feel the cold.

10: Monstrous Suggestions

Gable and its retinue were cloud-wrapped. Rain fell as though from a celestial hosepipe. Water glinted in the Tyson farmyard, but all was cosy within the house, where a log fire dispelled the damp. Tongues of flame brought answering flickers from the highly polished oakwork—from the spice cupboard, where in times past salt and other necessities were kept dry, from the big fitted dresser and from a doorway bearing the rippling effect of an adze.

The weather was "growy" this Sunday. Isaac Tyson, his wife Florrie, Aunt Ethel, Janet and Tony, mustered for one of the week's highlights in this very traditional household. It was Sunday Tea. Not quite as grand as when Grannie held sway, and everyone dressed up for the occasion, but thoroughly Cumbrian in the scones, with rum butter, home-made jam, fruit cake and tea kept warm in a pot enveloped in a knitted cosy.

Isaac Tyson kept to the old ways. There was electricity, but they didn't often use it. As Janet used to say, with a smile: "Dad switches the electricity on just to see his way to the paraffin lamp." Which happened on this occasion. Though it was summer, the light was poor and the lamp was lit. It gave a cosy feel to the room until it flickered and went out, blackening the glass.

"Thoo'll have to trim t'wick, mother," said Isaac. Which she did, performing the task by the light from a single 40 watt electric bulb which dangled from a central point. The room had been tidied up, for it was Sunday. In front of the fire lay the best pegged rug. The rack which could be raised or lowered, and was used for airing clothes (and, formerly, drying oatcake), was on this day idle, its wooden ribs bare.

A tin of salmon had been opened and, for once, the salmon had not been mixed with bread to make it go further. It was just as

Mr West, the canner, intended it to be used. There followed tinned pears—another great treat—the aforementioned scones and cake, to be consumed (one each) in that order.

It was usually a joyful occasion. A worthy Lakeland custom. Sunday Tea.

This time there was a feeling of unease. "That Monster thing's getting me down," said Isaac.

Jane remarked: "Henry says there must be someone in the dale who knows all about it."

"Oh—so it's Henry now," said Isaac.

Florrie, de-fusing a potential row, asked him to pass the rum butter.

Florrie did not think there was a Monster at all. "It's that chap John Thwaite, trying to drum up some trade."

Aunt Ethel settled for a big dog. A really big dog.

Isaac snorted: "With horns?"

Florrie kicked her husband under the table, which implied: "Be nice to Ethel."

Tony, who didn't usually have much to say, grunted: "Nobody had heard of a Monster till our American turned up."

Jane said: "Henry's hardly likely to import an animal new to science—which this one seems to be. There's some genetic disturbance..."

Aunt Ethel was impressed by the use of words. And by the first mention in the house of the American visitor.

"Oh, so it's Henry now?" said Ethel, echoing Isaac's words. She hadn't said much, but the effect was not far short of an exploding hand grenade. Tony stiffened and blustered. Jane remained cool on the surface but having a tangle of emotions within.

Sunday Tea resumed its normal routine of clinking crockery, the rush of well-broddled tea from a large teapot which had been pre-warmed, and the steady champing of Lakeland delicacies.

For a while, it had been quiet on the Media front. Reg occasionally included a gossip note about Monsters in the *Cumberland Gazette*. He didn't write a lot and tended to re-cycle what he had pasted in his little cutting book. His introductory sentences reflected a wide circle of friends. In fact, the "old Lakeland farmer" and the "Whitehaven housewife" were fictitious. They made just the right topical comment to enable Reg to re-use bits and pieces from the first Wassie article.

Reg and Miss Seed (it was still Miss Seed, not Mabel) were thinking of getting wed, to use the dale term for marriage. He had tried to persuade her to live with him, but Mabel Seed would not brook any Sinfulness. Reg sighed. It would have to be the Registry Office. He had grown to like Miss Seed and was addicted to her scones and fruit cake; to her selfless attitude and the tidy way she kept the office.

At Washolme, on that wet Sunday in springtime, Major Riseley was welcoming an emissary of the Channel Ten Natural History Unit, which had, to their viewers' considerable relief, lost interest in filming African beasties. The boredom factor extended to cheetahs chasing antelopes, which they never actually caught for fear of upsetting those who didn't like to see the television images splattered with blood, and hippos with repulsive habits in slimy pools.

A young but hard-bitten women researcher for Channel Ten, showing great courage, had trekked (motored!) beyond Watford and then Birmingham into an area which the natives called the Pennines. The adventurous journey was now extended to the north-west where, in an area of rain and cloud, she "discovered" lakes and mountains. And yet more natives. Were they friendly? The researcher, telephoning details of her progress to her boss in London, was asked to find out.

Daringly, she progressed through the district, finding there was organised life beyond Kendal and even beyond the high passes, as the natives called the roads which climbed through clouds. In Wasdale, she came across flocks of woolly animals called herdwicks. A Major Riseley had acted as interpreter when she mixed with local people. They did not speak recognisable English and had strange customs, like eating a dish called Tatie Pot and covering their scones with a mixture of rum and butter.

The researcher, well to the north of the range of cheetah and hippo, the standbys of the Natural History Unit, heard of the Wasdale Monster, a most fearsome beast.

Major Riseley had snorted when it was mentioned. "I cannot possibly believe that such a creature exists...Those who have seen it are the ones most addicted to the bottle," he told the researcher. And there the matter rested.

The whole thing had been an expensive exercise in doing nowt. On that wet Sunday in Wasdale, the researcher told Riseley that Channel Ten proposed to go back to its films about cheetahs chasing antelopes. The sponsors liked them. So did the biggest shareholder in Channel Ten, who had a whole cabinet of African wildlife films in his yacht, which had expensive moorings in the Caribbean.

In brief, Channel Ten had to think of its owners—and the ratings.

Nothing had changed.

Now it was summer. On the farms, two jobs clamoured for attention. The herdwicks must be clipped. And the grass cut and taken wind-and-sun dried as hay or green as silage.

Isaac remembered when clipping time in Wasdale was like a carnival. All the farmers came together and clipped at each farm in turn.

A dozen or so men had sat on lile wooden stools, specially made to hold a man and a sheep. And grasping and subduing a sheep like a wrestler, Cumberland and Westmorland style, a clipper went through the traditional routine of clipping off the fleece. The sheep was passed on to be re-marked, a sign of ownership, and the wool was folded and put in store until it was collected.

It was a great day, which ended with feasting and dancing, till milking time on the following morning.

"Nowt's t'same," Isaac lamented, for the umpteenth time, as he looked for a telephone number and rang up the contract-clippers.

What happened after that fair took his breath away.

A few lads arrived with a Land Rover and a trailer. And set about shearing by what one of them said was the Bowen technique. Isaac, with the help of Jane and the neighbour's lads, plus two or three dogs, had rounded up the sheep at first light. They came down the fell lane like a flow of grey lava and milled around the big croft, with the yows bleating and the lambs calling out incessantly as though proclaiming the end of the world.

One of the lads told Isaac he started clipping in the Falkland Islands and worked his way through Europe till he'd run out of

87

summer. Isaac, who was very much a local man, gave a long, low whistle of wonder. The lad laughed. "I was used to clipping hornless sheep. I didn't fancy holding a horned sheep between my legs—but now I do it!"

The clipping began. It was like watching a production line at a factory. Before a sheep had time to blink three times, it had lost its fleece. A lad spent no more than a minute or two with each animal; then, while he grabbed another sheep, he passed the previous one between his legs, whence it was sent on its way to a croft to be re-united with the (bemused) lambs.

They bleated all the louder when they saw the strange, shorn sheep. Something terrible had happened to mother!

Up at Gill Head, Owd Jack was haymaking. It was simplicity itself. With only a house-cow, he mowed a few acres by scythe. When it had dried off, it was shifted into the barn using an old peat cart.

His few hoggs, the youngsters of his little flock, had been down on the coastal marshes during the winter and, back at home, were thriving on the grass. Not that he could do much about them, for they were among the sheep affected by the Chernobyl fall-out.

His herdwick tups (or 'tips' as he preferred to call them) did nowt but eat and fatten in the best pasture. Jack was certainly a good-hand at breeding herdwicks. He couldn't remember what he'd had for breakfast, but he could look at a sheep and recall its antecedents through a dozen generations.

Major Riseley sat on the front lawn of his fellside home with the man who, he hoped, would solve some of the mysteries of the monster-wracked valley.

Professor Ernst Ock, a specialist on Mutation, and the author of a new book, *An Introduction to the Study of the Nervous System of an Irradiated Fluke-Worm,* was—with his spherical figure—just like the film-type German professor. His body was rounded. His head had sunk into it, for no neck was visible. He had a professorial forehead, broad and gleaming. Riseley, in a rare comic moment, thought the professor was like a rocket looking for a launch-pad to stand on.

The professor, who had come into Riseley's life when he was Somebody in the Ministry, had arrived in Wasdale on the

88

previous evening. He gave the impression he was entering a danger zone. He threw up his arms in horror at the sight of the impregnated card devised to kill nothing more sinister than house-flies. Ock declared the poison intended for flies had been developed from a nerve gas. Donning rubber gloves, supplied by Mrs Riseley, he carried the card into the garden for burial.

At dinner, he carefully removed every trace of fat from the meat for (as he said) the fall-out from atomic explosions and accidents tended to build up in the fatty tissues of herbivores.

Said the Major: "I think you'll find our English beef perfectly edible. This has come from a farm not more than two miles from here."

It was Owd Jack's farm. The Professor poked at the meat with his fork, noticing the complete absence of fat. He didn't like to tell his host that the beef was, indeed, well-hung venison.

The professor seemed to be obsessed by Chernobyl. He knew all about it and hinted darkly that we had not heard the last of that particular hell's kitchen and the polluted cloud which had swept much of Europe, sprinkling the good earth with—who knew what?

All this talk of Doomwatch seemed a world away from Wasdale on that mild day when clouds were building up over Gable and its neighbours like gigantic woolsacks and the fan-shaped dalehead was still astonishingly green. The only detectable pollution was an old familiar whiff of sheep-dip.

The professor said, in his gutteral East European voice, with a limited selection of English words: "Zem sheep-dips were discovered to be injurious to Nature. Zay were banned in case they caused nasty side-effects to ze farmers."

Mrs Risley said, chirpily: "No one seems to be worried about the effect on the sheep."

Her husband shushed her, for the ten thousandth time, and turned his face professorwards. He began to speak with the fervour of the enthusiast about the fate which lay in store for humanity. "Zis is caused by interfering wizz Nature." A trickle of words became a torrent as he warmed to his favourite topics of genetic practices, mutating microbes, ineffective antibiotics and, eventually, what seemed to be his favourite among the world's exotic diseases—ebola.

89

The professor brought from his pocket a small tin, which had started out life holding tobacco. He opened it to reveal cotton wool, on which reposed what appeared to be bilberries.

Said the professor: "Here is proof that animals can be affected."

Mrs Riseley picked up one of the bilberries and examined it while the professor went to his room. He returned with a geiger counter and said: "Zees are radio-active sheep droppings." The needle on the geiger counter drifted across the dial and there was a crackling.

The Riseleys paled in a matter of seconds.

The professor was just warming up. "Who knows what we will find? There'll be Mutants. Hybrids. Mongrels. "Ze men who look for dinosaurs find one every seven weeks."

"Do they keep losing it?" asked Mrs Riseley sweetly.

The professor, annoyed with her—and himself—continued: "...a different one every seven weeks. Half of all zee known dinosaur remains have been found in zee last two decades."

He paused, as though waiting for applause.

Mrs Riseley was not there to applaud. After dropping the "bilberry", she had dashed into the kitchen. For the next ten minutes, the tap water flowed and disinfectant was splashed about as she rid herself of traces of the professor's radio-active sheep-dirt, as she primly called it.

Before Riseley could ask for more information about what seemed a particular noxious ailment, his wife said, twitteringly: "Tea is going cold." She looked slightly worried as she turned to the professor and asked: "Are muffins safe?"

Riseley himself was becoming convinced that, if a Monster existed, there was "something in the air" which caused quite ordinary, innocent creatures to develop in size, stature and aggression. His wife yawned. The professor winced at the broad sweep of his simplications.

"Indeed," said Riseley, "the Wasdale Monster is nothing more than a quite ordinary herdwick tup which has mutated. I suggest, sir, that it is, no more, no less (and now he began to quote from the dictionary definition he had memorised) the occurrance of a new form differing from its parents as a result of change in the gene structure of a reproductive cell."

The professor began to shake—or, rather, wobble. He who disliked eating fat on meat had managed to swaddle himself comfortably in fat of his own making and was doubtless radioactive himself. Now the fat shivered and rolled. It was not a pretty sight. When things had subsided, the Major concluded that the professor had been laughing.

11: Salmon, Stag—and a Wife

When Henry arrived at the farm, Owd Jack was resting his elbows on the top bar of a gate, staring appreciatively at a group of fine herdwick tups.

Though it was a hot day, and Jack had cast his jacket, he was still swaddled in clothes—vest, thick flannel shirt, though with sleeves rolled up. As it was not a formal occasion, like going to t'auction, Jack was not wearing a collar. A metal collar-stud caught the eye of the sun. And Jack was wearing his thick trousers, held up by gallases, as he called braces.

Said the farmer: "I'd rayther look at a good tup than a pretty woman..." He neutralised his remark by winking.

Henry was impressed by the quality of the animals, and especially by what appeared to be the best of a good bunch—the patriarch of the fell, with white face, rough like hoar-frost, well-shaped head from which horns protruded like battering rams.

They were spirited animals, but slow to rouse. A tup which had been penned clearly wanted to be out and back on the fell. It did not get het-up, as Jack would have said, but stood there, apparently with a mental vacuum until—THWACK! The tup lunged forward and smacked the top bar of the pen.

From a nearby poultry hut came a thumping sound. "That's t'auld tup," said Jack, adding: "Grandfadder—so to speak. I browt it up in yon hut. It was nobbut a lile lamb when it's mother dropped it there. She deed. I nivver got round to mothering it on. Just fed it wi' spare milk. Talk about thrive! Then I fixed up a few baulks of wood to play with when it felt frisky. That's what you can hear now."

The thumping sound was resumed. Henry smiled at the thought of a sheep being reared in a wooden hut.

Jack was not eager to change the topic. "T'back wall o' yon hut is so thin, it'd go through if yon animal leaned on it. Do you know what's keeping it in?"

Henry shook his head.

"It's psychology, lad. It doesn't knaw it can git oot." Jack wheezed. It was another round of laughter. Jack was quiet for a moment, then said: "Thoo wean't tell anybody. I don't want a lot o' gawpers up here."

"Honest—I won't tell a soul."

Jack said: "I'm going to take you in hand, Henry lad. Tha needs a wife."

"Thus speaks a crusty old bachelor."

"Don't mock me. My folk were always slow starters. Must have been a bit of Irish blood in us somewhere. My old father used to tell me he was a slow starter. If a girl had looked at him, he'd hev run a mile. And when one told t'other kids he was her boy friend, he coloured up like beetroot."

"But he made it in the end."

"Aye, lad. It's just that he needed a bit o' pushing."

"Who pushed?"

"Ma!" Jack wheezy laugh reminded Henry of someone trying to kick-start a motor bike.

"They were courting ten year."

"So." Jack didn't like to waste words.

"So," echoed Henry, tucking his checked shirt into the top of his denims as he prepared to leave.

Jack reflected—as indeed the herdwick tup was doing before continuing its splinter-campaign against the pen. "Afore this year is out, Henry lad, you'll have done what my owd dad did long years ago. Within twelve month, he'd gaffed a salmon, shot

92

a red stag—and snared a wife. In that order!''

Henry, who now had the hang of local speech, said "Appen."

The salmon were "running". A shiver of excitement passed up the dale when the first one was seen, being dragged along the river bank by Simeon's lile dog. There was the usual talk of one of the urban gangs turning up to dynamite the best pools, so Geordy McGlen, the water bailiff, and PC Hoggarth, the local constabulary—bless him!—were on full alert.

Major Riseley, avid reader of *Country Style* and other trade journals, prepared to welcome selected guests for a spell of salmon fishing on the local reaches, which were owned by the Swartz Trust. Riseley, whose collective assets were £39.00 in the Post Office Savings Account, loved spending other people's money. In this case, the Trust would pay. He made sure there were one or two military titles and the odd OBE among those guests. A list of the celebrities would be posted to the *Cumberland Gazette*.

This was Riseley at his most expansive, sitting with his guests in the drawing room of Washolme, while Colleen, the agency maid, went round with the drinks and brought a touch of glamour to the scene. She was proving to be a little too glamorous, diverting attention from the lord and master. He must insist on someone plain next time.

When she flashed Riseley a smile, her eyes seem to have an inner light source. "Will that be all?" she asked, turning on her high heels and clicking out of the room, the guests following with undisguised interest the ripples of her hour-glass figure.

Riseley stood by the big fireplace, which appeared to be made of marble, but was actually painted slate—not too well painted, and looking like marmalade. He had acquired two sporting dogs to adorn the hearthrug. They were setters of a rusty hue. One of them kept grunting as it slept, doubtless chasing hares and grouse across the fields and moors of its mind. The other seemed to have a bone stuck in its mouth.

The log fire crackled and put on a display of shooting sparks. The long case clock was tickless, being used to store Riseley's rod and tackle. He had seen it used so in an old film. The idea had taken his fancy. The furnishings in the room had about them a touch of faded grandeur.

93

"May I welcome you to this old Lakeland estate," said Riseley. "I promise that if we have salmon for dinner, it will not have come out of a tin." It was the nearest he had ever come to being funny.

This year, Gerald the television tycoon was on the guest list. He certainly looked the part, thanks to the Summit Television costume department. As he looked round the room, he was already planning to "shoot" a costume drama here. Maybe *Jane Eyre.*

One of his friends, an American director, had made him wince recently by remarking: "Who is this dame called Charlotte Bronte? I've only seen two of her films."

Gerald strode around the room, ever restless and forever looking through a frame formed of the fingers of his hand.

Also present (as the social magazines have it) was Captain Strickle, not so much one of Riseley's Army friends as his only Army friend. It was his first visit to the Lake District. He found similarities between the area and Nepal, where he had served his country, bringing law and order to the natives.

The third guest was proving to be an embarrassment. He was an entertainer called Shush, of the pop group *Gayclops,* a man dripping with money who had estates in several parts of Britain. A highly restless man, Shush was a great chewer of gum and goodness knows what else. His face was drip-white, as though his blood was seeping away. He spoke a sort of Liverpool American, frequently using the word "man" to round off a sentence.

"Say, man..."

"I beg your pardon," said Riseley.

"That painting. Who did it, man?"

"It's a Constable."

"Gee."

Shush was so enraptured by the painting (which was, in truth, a good reproduction of a rural scene) he managed to stop chewing gum for a while.

"It's a good painting." Riseley felt he must keep the conversation ticking over.

"You can say that again," said Shush. "He's a good artist. Look at the way he's covered all the numbers up."

94

Shush had arrived with a dog handler and selection of animals, two genuine Scottish ghillies, his manager, agent, technician and a mobile recording studio, from which came sounds not unlike that of dustbins being rolled down steps. The shrill rather than the meek were about to inherit the earth, thought Riseley.

"Say..."

"Pardon?"

"Do we have a crack at the Monster? This Wassie thing? When I was in the States recently, it was mentioned on the telly."

Riseley sighed. He would have preferred a better class of visitor.

Geordy, forever a Scot, despite many years of domicile in England, had several hats. He was a man of medium height, tweedily dressed, with side-whiskers poking from beneath the sides of his deer-stalker hat, in this case a mark of his calling. For George was deer warden, head gardener and foreman of the Swartz Trust estate. When he was not working he was in his bothy, as he called his neat estate home, to the annoyance of his wife, sipping whisky, reading old copies of *Scots Magazine*, and listening to sad Heiland airs.

Riseley insisted that he went to the Women's Institute to talk about his work, and especially about salmon, confident he would have some kind words to say about his master. Geordy fortified himself with a few drams and rashly invited the ladies to interject if they had something pertinent to say.

Nature, said Geordy, is wonderful. "Wee salmon leave the river and swim all the way to the deep water off Greenland, where they feed until they are bloated. Then they return to their auld hame to breed."

"It seems a lot o' trouble," observed one of the women.

"Aye," conceded Geordy, "but they've bin doing it a long time. It suits 'em. And do you know, a salmon can find its own river—by the smell!"

The chairman of the Women's Institute, who was never quiet for long, said: "I wouldn't like to smell some of t'rivers after they've had a dose of chemicals and silage juice."

One member, whose only association with salmon was via the John West cannery, said: "I don't see why yon fish bother to

95

come back here. Why don't they stay where t'food's good and just swim round and round till they die?''

Geordy sighed. "They've got to breed, wumman. And when they're full of eggs, there's no room for food. So they dinna eat.''

The inquirer, overcome by the wonder of it all, simply said: "Just fancy!'' She counted ten and changed the subject to some raw local gossip. "I see Tony Dunderpate has been warming up some old broth again.'' (He had returned to one of his old girl friends).

The chairman brought the meeting to order.

"What about t'Monster?'' asked a farmer's wife. "We've had some more sheep savaged.''

Geordy sighed. "I've never seen it.''

The farmer's wife rasped: "I've never seen a giraffe, lad, but I'll tell you now, without fear of contradition—there is such a thing as a giraffe.''

The meeting ended with a flurry of speculation about the appearance of the Gingerish Thing which periodically terrorised the dale.

Geordy escaped without having to judge the monthly competition, which was for the best poem about jam-making. He stood for a few moments outside the hall, breathing deeply, then strode to his wee bothy. Soon he was in the pre-bedtime routine of bath and wee drammy. He lowered his ageing Scottish frame on to his bed and entered his womanless dream-world of glens, pines, capercaillies, stags and drams—lots of drams, for whisky was not just a drink, it was a medicine and also the Water of Life.

Meanwhile, Operation Salmon was underway. Owd Jack alerted Jane, who called to see Henry. She grimaced at the disarray in the cottage and at the ancient food smells. "Be at the Brokken Bridge near Washolme. Midnight. Wear dark clothes. Bring a torch.''

To languid Henry, who was never at his best before noon, it sounded like a message from a Hollywood spy film. Jane departed at speed, her car radio crackling out yet another summons to an ailing beast.

A little short of midnight, the moon hung over Wasdale. Movements might be detected at t'Brokken Bridge, which leapt across the river in a single jubilant span. Jack, Jane and Henry

96

startled each other by arriving stealthily on foot. The first two had left their cars a good way from the river. Henry got a lift to a point near Washolme by a late reveller from the *Woolsack*.

Henry, his footsteps muffled by the suede shoes he habitually wore, walked beside the owl-haunted beeches. He stood for a while, looking at the silhouette of the old house, blocky against a sky illuminated by the cold light of the moon. If it had been daylight, you would have had a better view of his smile.

Nothing stirred apart from a roe deer, which had been grazing on the lawn, and the whisky which Henry carried in a hip-flask—as a medicine, of course.

Geordy's cottage was in darkness. The water-bailiff lay on his back, exhaling carbon dioxide and whisky fumes. The air around the house was fragrant with woodsmoke from a fire which refused to die.

Jack, who had left his old banger of a van in Seward's Barn, carried a torch and a gaff—a nasty pronged weapon. Lumbering along behind him was the dog he used at sheepdog trials. He had trained it not to bark, even if somebody trod on its foot.

Jane, wearing skin-tight clothes, which enhanced her slim body, had used up some of her surplus nervous energy by running most of the way from home.

When Henry first saw the gaff, the weapon to be employed for catching a salmon, he winced and felt sorry for any fish which would be at the receiving end. Jack had every intention of stabbing the luckless creature, which would be attracted by the light being played on the water.

They were sworn to silence. "On a neet like this, t'local bobby could hear your heart beatin at fifty paces..."

There was no special river sound. The water ran through a series of pools, the banks of which were lagged with sand. When a wood owl gave a "kewick" sound, Henry almost jumped out of his wellies. It was, said Jack, a female telling her offspring to clear off. They must not darken the door of the nesting hole again.

Jane, who had been poaching salmon with Jack in previous years, said: "Grandad used a biscuit tin with a hole in it. He had a candle for the light."

Jack said: "Shussh." The others tittered at the thought of the famous pop star who was sleeping at the big house.

Jack chose a place where the flow was slack and the pool shadowed by a riverside alder. Soon the torch was in play. He gave a low whistle, his signal for Henry to join him. Henry wore wellies. He felt the pressure of water against them and hoped the rims would remain above river level.

Jack, holding the lamp steady, showed Henry where their quarry was lying. It was a huge salmon, its body in continuous motion as it held its place at the edge of a big pool. Henry, lost in wonder at the sheer beauty of the fish, had temporarily forgotten the business in hand.

Jack handed him the gaff. Henry shuddered and handed it back. Jack returned it, covered Henry's grasp with his own calloused hand and brought the gaff down with a crunch.

Fifteen pounds of indignant fish churned the water into foam. Henry, in his excitement, called out. In an instant, he was waist deep in the pool, though still holding the gaff, which had the salmon connected to its barb.

There was a deafening silence. Jane and Jack froze like herons and listened for any responsive sounds. They came within seconds. Geordy's dogs began a round of barking. They could imagine the water-bailiff groaning as he clambered from his bed.

The fatally-wounded salmon seemed to realise the enormity of the crime which Henry had committed. For a few moments it stopped flapping.

A rearguard action was soon underway. It began in an orderly fashion. Jack slipped the salmon into a sack. The gaff was concealed under a bush and would be collected later. Jack led the way downriver, to a place under t'Brokken Bridge. Henry shivered until Jack slung his old overcoat over him. The dogs had stopped barking. Geordy's voice must have quietened them.

They heard the rasp of shoes against the road—two pairs of shoes—and a mumble of voices. Henry tingled with excitement at the prospect of being caught poaching salmon. He was smiling again.

The strangers stopped, half way across the bridge. A man's voice said: "Stop blubbering." A woman cried even louder and was silenced by someone giving her a sharp slap.

98

Said the man: "It isn't t' first time a girl's got into trouble. And it won't be the last." The voice was hard, unfeeling.

"Will you marry me?"

"Nay, I've never said I'd marry you."

"But I thought. . ."

"You know what thought did."

The sobbing was resumed.

"Here, I must go. You get back to the house. I'll keep in touch—and send you some money nearer the time."

He strode off.

The young woman gave an anguished cry and set off towards Washolme.

Under the bridge, Jack said: "I could break yon chap's bluddy back."

Henry, shocked at the callous manner, kicked a waterside thistle.

Jane said nothing. But she recognised the voices. The girl was the dark-haired lass who worked for the Riseleys. The man was—Tony.

No one wanted the salmon. The fun had lain in outwitting it and also Geordy, whose dogs were now off the lead, judging by their joyous cries.

Jack, with another of his famous winks, carried the big fish to the back of Washolme and tied it to the sneck on the kitchen door. Then the trio melted into the night. Jane gave Henry a lift to his cottage. Then she was gone. Mercifully, the radio was silent. She might get a couple of hours sleep before another working day began.

When Major Riseley had breakfasted and was ready to resume his estate duties, and uphold the law in this wild little dale, he had difficulty in opening the back door of the house. Leaving by another door, he walked round the building.

The first cold ray of sunlight was reflected back from the body of a fresh-run salmon, which was hanging from the latch. And with the salmon was a note, written in a hand unfamiliar to him, but undoubtedly that of a local farmer: "Tak me and say nowt."

What hurt the Major was not so much that his wife, when she heard, gave one of her tittering calls, but that his guests should know about it. And, if he was any sort of judge of human nature,

99

the tale would soon be joining tales of the Monster on the local rounds. The Major was never again heard to bluster on about salmon-poaching.

When Henry and Jack met next, the talk was about bagging a stag. Henry had been a good shot in America but had not handled a rifle for a few years.

Said Owd Jack: "I've marked the map for you. Look—theer's the valley where a few deer lie. If you go t'long way, you'll not get within half a mile. But take Sudden Death."

Jack's grimy finger pointed to a place on the map where the contour lines were so close together it looked like a diagram for electrical circuitry. "That's Sudden Death. Straight up. It'll save you miles."

Henry smuggled the gun back to his cottage and spent an evening with the map and a guide book. Jack's suggested route was up Nevvy Rake, a rocky path with a forty-five degree angle, and Nevvy (so twas said) had been a distiller of illegal whisky who had a still in a cave up there. It seems that one of his best customers was a magistrate who, when Nevvy was caught, usually paid his fine so there would be no interruption in the whisky supply.

It was still dark when Henry left the cottage for Nevvy's Rake. There had been a frost. Fallen leaves were crunchy under his feet. The sound was like someone eating corn flakes. Henry knew enough about the district to move without using a torch. He followed Nevvy's old track, up between the birch trees which, as daylight seeped into the dale, looked ghostly with their silver and black trunks.

Looking ahead, he saw the crags rimmed with pink sunlight. A buzzard circled and mewed. He had his first rest where the path tilted and began to zig-zag at the bottom of Nevvy Rake.

A clear voice cut through the morning-fresh air. "You take your time."

Jane was sitting on a lichened boulder, drinking from a thermos flask.

Henry's heartbeat quickened.

She poured him some coffee.

Neither of them spoke. They simply smiled at each other and resumed the climb. Up, up, up, at times slithering, at times

100

resting, with heaving lungs. Once they held hands for a moment. Actions speak louder than words.

They were thankful that Owd Jack had gathered his sheep for dipping, leaving the fell country silent, except for buzzard-mewing and the cry of an old carrion crow—a call which sounded like the honking of a vintage motor horn. They slithered over the rim of the crag and, still keeping low, found themselves among the rushes above Raven Crag.

The tinkle of beck water ensured that the deer were conditioned to a measure of sound. Henry marvelled at the effect of morning sunlight on the vermilion berries of a rowan which had rooted among stones near the beck.

The final approach to the herd would be under under cover of a drystone wall. But first they lay, waiting for the sound waves to settle. The October morning was calm and quite mild. They heard the roar of a red deer stag. The performance was not sustained. As Jane said, there is nothing like a touch of frost to get the rut under way.

The use of the word "roar" amused Henry. The sound was deep but more like a cow bawling to be milked than that of the Monarch of the Dale.

Jane nudged Henry. She was facing a large area of rushes. Just beyond stood a big stag, and they could see the heads of its harem—five, perhaps even six, hinds, with one or two calves of the year. Henry noticed the thick neck, the leonine mane and the redness of the coat, where it was not covered with peaty-mud from the wallowing. This stag, dirty and dishevelled, looked like a Rugby forward on a wet day. A tatter of thistle dangled from one of the stag's antlers, having been caught up in a frenzy of threshing.

As another stag approached, the big boy stood with head up-tilted, so that the antlers were almost brushing its back, and once again gave voice. The mouth opened until the void formed the letter O. The husky voice drifted across the uplands.

Henry lined his gun on the master stag. Jane said: "Spare him. Look for a little stag. It will have a blocky body."

Henry shifted his attention to the animal which had the temerity to challenge the master stag. He put pressure on the trigger, looking around for a few moments to assess the situation. The

101

master stag, a Royal, was perturbed. Perhaps a wraith of human scent had reached it. The stag ran its tongue over its nostrils to improve its scenting ability. With the hinds nearby, a dozen pairs of ears; a dozen noses, formed an effective Early Warning System. As they chewed the cud, only the tops of their heads were visible above the reeds.

The smaller stag stood for a moment, looking at the master. Henry's moment had arrived. The gun uttered a crack which brought an answering echo from the crags on the far side of the dale.

Hinds and calves of the year came rapidly to their feet. They were in full flight within seconds. Crows which had been languidly feeding at the start of a new day almost leapt out of their feathers and departed with sharp cries of alarm. The big stag went loping away. A sheep missed in Owd Jack's gather stamped on the ground in its annoyance.

In the dale, three men heard the sound of the rifle and responded in their various ways. Geordy, having been outwitted over the salmon, was now determined to catch the deer poachers. He had the local bobby with him. Owd Jack left his van in a lile quarry and set off up the valley. He had taken the precaution of daubing cow-muck on the number plates in case someone saw him making his get-away. A local would instantly recognise his two-tone van—blue and rust.

In that fraction of a second during which a bullet sang through the air, Henry and Jane stared at the departing deer. "I'm sure I had something in the sights," said Henry. "It's got to be dead."

They broke cover and advanced along the line the bullet had taken. The young stag, shot through the heart, must have been dead before it hit the ground. There was no trace of the bullet, which could have travelled another half mile. Henry shivered at the thought.

Thirty yards away, what looked at first glance to be a heap of sacking among the rushes resolved itself into the body of a large hairy creature with horns as strong as those of a buffalo. Its lips were curled, as though at the point of death this creature had evil thoughts.

Said Jane: "Here's a trophy for you! Wassie himself!"

102

"Gee".

Henry began to drag the body towards a scree slope. Jane helped him to conceal it.

"Now for the stag," she said.

"Leave it."

"We'll be caught."

"I'll be caught. You leave now. Take the gun. It's Jack's. If I know that old ruffian, he won't have a licence for it. Cross the valley. Drop down to where Jack will be waiting."

"And you?"

"Fret not thyself—as the Good Book says."

Jane shivered. Both had been so absorbed by the climb and the stalk, they had not realised the morning had a nip in the air. Henry encircled Jane with his arms. She snuggled. Then laughed. For a moment, Henry thought she was laughing at him.

He looked anxiously down at her face.

"I'm happy."

They snuggled again, as a red sun turned to cream and assumed mastery of the sky. The rushes arched their backs in the breeze. A dog yapped at one of the dale farms. Otherwise there was silence.

Jane laughed again and said: "I've just been reading a soppy love story as a change from *Cattle in Health and Sickness.*"

"Hmmm," said Henry. It was a situation in which feelings mattered more than words. They kissed several times, then languidly.

Said Jane: "I can't help thinking of that soppy novel. The hero clasped a firm young body."

"So have I."

"And felt the pounding of her heart..."

"Of course."

"Have I got firm young breasts?"

"I'll have a look."

She laughed, pushed him away. They kissed again. And she was gone, melting into the landscape.

A curtain of cloud was drawn across the sun. When it found a hole in the canopy, the world coloured up again. Sunlight played across the valley with the intensity of a searchlight. Henry leaned against a lichen-plated boulder and sighed with contentment.

His gaze went down the fellside to the dale, which was like a green fingermark on the landscape. He saw the semi-ruined walls and outbuildings in which an earlier generation had taken such pride. A few beef cattle lumbered across the old grazing land.

He also thought of a certain firm young body and found himself musing about the appearance of the breasts.

When Geordy and the policemen were close, Henry called to them. They should have been warned by his manner that things were not quite as they seemed.

The two men sank thankfully down beside him. Geordy wheezed a little. The policeman, who came from town, loosened some of the buttons on his tunic.

Geordy had been prepared for a shouting match with the poacher. Instead, he was affable. He'd met many a worse man than this quiet American, with his rucksack, from which he drew a thermos flask, offering his guests some coffee.

For once in his career, the policeman did not know when to begin the official business. Then he said lamely: "Did you shoot this stag?"

"Sure."

"You're a cool 'un."

They left the stag on the hill. Geordy had no intention of dragging it down. He would return with one of the all-terrain vehicles which had taken over from the pony when there were deer to be taken down to the larder.

An hour later, sweating profusely, they were at Washolme, standing in the presence of Major Riseley, who was also a magistrate and now had a real, live, breathing deer poacher in custody. He was proud of himself.

His little wife reserved judgement—and her famous titter. For pride cometh before a fall.

"Did you shoot this deer?" asked the policeman.

"Yes."

"Why?"

"Because it's mine." It was said quietly but had the explosive force of an exploding shell.

Riseley, looking and sounding pompous, remarked: "In this part of the world we have not yet got round to common ownership."

104

Riseley's wife tried to rub from her face a crease of merriment.

The policeman said: "I must caution you..."

Said Henry: "Perhaps I should first give you my name."

"Pardon, sir, but Major Riseley has furnished that information. Henry Kilkoff."

"My real name is Swartz."

Another verbal shell exploded.

Riseley went white.

His wife tittered.

Henry said: "Ring up Grannie Swartz in New York and you'll find I've just shot one of my own stags. She gave Wasdale to me as a coming-of-age present...Oh, and I've also shot the Monster. It's just a great big ragged herdwick tup."

There wasn't much more to be said. Henry sounded so convincing that his story was accepted without question. Geordy had his job to think about. Riseley was keen to maintain his status. The policeman was relieved to be able to return to civilisation.

At the first opportunity, Henry slipped on to the fell with a pair of sheep-clippers. He found the corpse of the Monster and, using the shears, cut away the tinted initials JH. He'd often wondered why Jack should have been so secretive about his herdwicks.

Henry sliced the body open and left it on the fell as food for the foxes and the ravens. It would keep a raven's stomach as tight as a drum for a week or two.

Henry dashed over to Owd Jack's house to report.

"Salmon, deer—but I doubt there'll be a bride."

Henry chilled.

Said Jack: "When she heard who you really were, it was as bad as if someone had chucked a bucketful of beck-watter over her."

"And..."

"She's gone. Left the dale. I wouldn't go and see Isaac, if I were you. He's fuming."

Henry returned to the cottage in the woods. The reds and blues and yellows of life had become a general grey. He mustered just enough mental energy to complete his record of local life. Said Owd Jack, on one of his rare visits: "Nay, lad, what does ta want to spend all thee time poking about in t'deeard past for?" Henry found it too much of an effort to reply.

Another Wasdale winter was upon them. There was no word of Jane. Henry kept away from the big house. He wanted nothing to do with estate affairs. There was consolation in visiting places where he had been close to Jane. On one of his high fell walks, near the crags where the ravens were nesting, Henry came across a flock of snow buntings. The buntings, with their jingling voices, were trying to infuse a little life into the bleak landscape.

The frost intensified. Sheep were brought down to the fields, to be fed on precious hay. The song of the beck became muted. Waterfalls set hard with frills of icicles. With the Monster dead, something of the sparkle had gone from local life. Regular customers at the *Woolsack* did not know what to talk about.

Spring was tardy. Then the new season's warmth enveloped the dale and fought its way to the heights. Bees visited patches of purple saxifrage. On the mosses, the herdwicks plucked at the "mosscrop", as the dale farmers called cotton-grass in its early stage of growth.

Winter remained in the heart of Isaac Tyson, who was lamenting the decline of his native dale and still annoyed that this young American should have played fast and loose with the affections of his daughter (to quote one of Grannie's old phrases).

Spring came with the chacking of wheatears and the cool, clear song of the cock ring-ouzel from the crags. Jack called the bird a northern nightingale. Warmth seeped into the recesses of the fells.

Jack told Henry that Jane was working in Borrowdale. On impulse, Henry set off to see her. He made no preparation. His feet moved like automata. For clothing, he had just what he stood up in. And he had no idea where the next meal would come from.

He understood what the herdwick ewe felt when, having been sold and moved to another part of the district, she trekked across country to her native patch of fell. His feet found the rock-strewn path from Wasdale to Sty Head. He was under the gaze of Great Gable and saw splashes of colour—the rainbow hues of clothing worn by visitors.

The wheatears kept him company. They were at home on boulder-strewn ground where rabbit burrows made ideal nesting sites. Henry watched a cock bird on a boulder flirt its wings

106

and gave a hard call, like two stones being clashed together.

Henry, absorbed with thoughts about Jane, did not notice the chilling of the air with increased height, nor the blue-black cloud spreading from the south-west and soon to overtake him. Henry saw climbers dangling from Nape's Needle and was overtaken at speed by some runners in shorts. A wind sprang up from nowhere. He shivered.

With an image of Jane in his mind, he had no thoughts of turning back. Then Sty Head Tarn came into view. It was dull grey, like old pewter. The flanking fells were darkening by the minute at the onset of a storm. He saw the mountain rescue box, like a coffin on stilts. As the first, fat raindrops bounced off the hard ground he slipped into the box. The lid shut with a clunk.

It was a timely action. The rain fell with the intensity of water from a celestial hosepipe. A little water seeped into the crowded box, but otherwise Henry was dry. The storm passed, rampaging over Borrowdale. Henry shivered with fear when his first efforts to extricate himself from this wooden box were unsuccessful. Then he shivered because he had little to wear and because he had not eaten since breakfastime.

What seemed like hours later, he heard a creak as someone sat on the box. What was Henry to do? Should he thump on the box, then speak, asking the newcomer to open it? He might be scared and clear off.

"Excuse me." Henry's voice was squeaky with fear and concern.

There was no response.

"Please—let me out of the box."

He heard someone fumbling with the fixtures. The door swung open—and Henry, cramped and weary, staggered out and sat on the rocks, taking in great draughts of air.

His saviour was a young man, as thinly attired and as cold as he was. They sat, side by side, waiting for strength to return to their stiff limbs. Each was exhausted. The stranger said: "I should have been back in Borrowdale hours ago. The storm held me up. Then I wandered about."

"I expected you to dash off when I spoke," said Henry.

"I hadn't got the energy!"

Henry, having been released from the box, now set about

107

helping the lad who had rescued him. They limped along the rough track towards Stockley Bridge, and had almost arrived when the rescue team met them. The first intimation came with the raucous voice of a car siren and flashing lights from the dale far below. Half a dozen volunteers, with bright orange outer clothing, ropes, survival gear and stretchers, appeared.

Henry noticed with a smile that almost all the men were relatively small, stocky, bearded, as though they had been specially selected for the work. They used modern technology to infuse warmth into chilled and damp limbs. Then Henry and the other walker were lifted on to stretchers for the short journey down to Seathwaite Farm, where the team's base had been established.

Henry, having dozed, awoke to find himself in the farm kitchen. Someone was leaning over him. When his eyes focussed, that someone was revealed as Jane, a vet with a part-time commitment to mountain rescue. She looked far too young for such work. She also looked concerned. Said Jane to Henry: "I'd better come back to Wasdale. It looks as though you can't manage without me."

And Henry slipped happily back into the sleep of someone utterly exhausted by his day's walk.

They were married at Wasdale Church on a day which began with rain and mist. As Owd Jack said: "I reckon t'day looks as if it's bin up all neet." Jane, who early on the morning of her wedding day was called out to an emergency, had her hand up a cow's backside when recovering a dead twin calf.

The Weather Clerk relented, calling up a wind to blow the cloud and mist away. Wasdale had never looked more appealing when Jane arrived, only twenty minutes later and not, as rumour had it, wearing white wellies.

Henry was attired (Miss Seed's phraseology) in morning dress (in deference to his father, Jabez Swartz II, who were similarly clad). Grannie was unable to attend the wedding, but promised to drop in at the first opportunity. Henry's sister, Rebecca, the celebrated Girl in Red of the Wasdale dance, returned, again wearing red, and attracted almost as much attention as the bride.

Simeon said: "There must be life in this old dog. My glasses have steamed up."

Rebecca gave him a smacking kiss, leaving a smear of lipstick across one of his cheeks. It gave the impression of capillary bleeding.

Jane had persuaded her father to wear his best-setting off suit, which turned out to be the one he had been married in thirty years before. It was woefully out-of-date, having buttonholes on the jacket and turn-ups on the trousers. So he was shamed into going to Whitehaven, where he hired morning dress.

The church bell clanged. Henry and his best man, Jonty Gill, were half an hour early. They sat in the snug little church, staring at the stained glass. Henry later said he would be able to paint a picture of that glass—every fine, irregular piece of stained glass—without further reference to it. They were also weary of listening to the harmoniumist playing Handel's *Largo*—over and over again, for the full thirty minutes.

Owd Jack turned up in a suit which was dreadfully out of date and smelt of moth-balls.

All the dalesfolk were determined to attend. Kids ran up and down the aisle and swung on the bellrope. Jane's mother was heard to say to Isaac, during the lull, "You should have gone before we came."

When the parson was heard to ask Henry if he took Jane to be his lawfully wedded wife, Owd Jack muttered, from the back pew, that "t'lad's come o' purpose". Jennie Scarr, the organist, had a cap which matched the pulpit fall.

The children tied up the churchyard gate and would not untie it until there had been the customary scramble for small change.

The Riseleys were invited to the reception, for Swartz family reasons, and the Tysons managed to be civil—just for the day! The two women got on so well that before the day was over they were exchanging recipes. Florrie Tyson was invited to tea at the big house where, as a servant lass, she had laboured long and hard for a shilling a week, with keep. She insisted on being shown the lile attic room where three servant lasses had slept.

Madge Seed, writing up the wedding for the *Cumberland Gazette*, somewhat spoiled the image of poshness by mentioning the reception, at the bride's house—as an event held in a tent. She should have written "marquee", which gave a better idea of its size and opulence. No expense was spared to feed the multitude.

109

Isaac complained: "I've nivver stopped writing cheques since our Jane said she was to be wed."

The happy couple were intending to stay at the big house overnight, then drive off into the sunset on the following day.

Their plans were changed by a radio message: "Base to Vet Five. Base to Vet Five."

"Vet Five to Base. Over."

"Base to Vet Five. Congratulations and good wishes. And there's an emergency at Mr Dyson's, Lane Head. There's no one else to attend to it."

"Vet Five to Base. Going right away. Over."

She said to Henry, as she left the reception, having hastily donned shirt, jeans and wellies: "See you sometime, love."

Said Henry: "Husband to Wife. Message Received. Over. For the time being."

12: Wasdale Show

October in Wasdale. The bracken took on its bronze shade, a delight for visiting photographers. Norse raiders, fieldfares and redwings—bird immigrants from Scandinavia—ran amok, stripping redberries from the rowans. The ground was blotched as though with drops of blood.

Now that the human visitors had departed for their winter quarters, the native life came back into its own. The main event was the Wasdale Show.

Henry and Jane awoke in Owd Jack's cottage. Their bridal bed had not arrived in time. They occupied a kingsize sleeping bag on the floor. Parked outside was the car with the crackly radio, decorated overall with toilet rolls. A mobile phone lay beside the makeshift bed. Someone had written on the mirror: "Dust me".

Owd Jack's wedding present was a second-hand fridge, in which reposed two objects—a gobbet of venison and a tin of baby powder. There was a note: "Salmon, stag, wife—now what?"

Down at Washolme, Major Riseley dressed slowly, carefully, for as President of the Wasdale Show he must set an example. He had a feeling it was going to be a special day for him. His wife had resolved not to titter.

A dustbin-rolling-down-the-steps sound from the Old Coach House indicated that special guests, Shush and the *Gayclops*, were back in the dale, eager to take part in the Show. They'd heard a rumour that Prince Charles might be there. Their normal £20,000 fee would be waived. It would do their image no harm at all if they hob-nobbed with Royalty.

Reg and Mabel (for such it was, and they had the "marriage lines" to prove it) awoke in a new flat. Two press tickets for the Wasdale Show were propped against the clock. Reg closed his eyes again. When he returned to consciousness, breakfast was ready, and his show-suit was laid out on the spare bed, and Mabel was there—wife, cook, pipe-cleaner and part-time reporter. He knew he had not been cut-out for bachelordom.

Summit Television sent their Outside Broadcast Unit to the Show. What matter if a rumour was circulating that the Monster had been shot? There was no evidence yet. What matter if the gateway to the showfield was too narrow for their cumbersome Outside Broadcast trucks? Taking down a few yards of wall was a modest charge to defray.

Gerald, ensuring he would get interesting pictures, had hired a pseudo-Monster for the day. This monster walked upright, was about the size of a man and, when it/he breathed out, the smell of stale ale was evident.

Everyone was in bubbling good spirits. There was a wash of Lakeland speech, with lots of yans and gurts, the odd thrang and a single miff-maff when somebody was thought to be talking a lot o' nonsense. Greetings were shouted at a range of a hundred yards. Affability abounded. Isaac Tyson, nodding in the Major's direction, remarked: "There's no show wi'out Punch."

A jolly stick-maker told inquirers he had been making crooks and sticks for forty years. His design was the standard one— ram's horn and hazel. "Where do you get the hazel?" asked a visitor. "Off hazel bushes." He gave another jolly laugh.

Everyone was out-shouted by the man at the mike. He announced a race for children. When the entrants had gathered, he handicapped them, beginning with the words: "Who's got t'shortest legs? You! Have a long start. Come on. . ." A pause. The booming voice continued: "When I say 'go; you run like. . .(another pause). You run fast!"

Shush and the *Gayclops* opened up with their revival of the old song, *It must be Jelly, cos Jam don't Shake like That.* The semicircle of high fells acted like a giant echo-chamber. "Gee", said Shush, most impressed. "Gee—what a gorgeous hunk of scenery, Man."

Simeon said: "After that din, I've no fear of hell."

Isaac said it was a toss up which he hated most—pop music, vacuum cleaners or low-flying aircraft.

A hound trail was announced. Someone referred to dogs and was corrected with the words: "Them's hoonds." A Sabbatical hush descended on the field as the man with the drag appeared at a distant wall and waited for the signal to advance, laying the last of the aniseed-and-oil trail on the sappy grass.

As he began to run towards us, a medley of "hoond" cries were heard. A tawny tide of animals swept past him. Seconds later, the animals were clambering over a wall. Yelps of frustration were heard from animals which had not made a clean passage. A line of hounds swept up the fellside beyond.

Forty minutes (and ten miles) later, t'hoonds were back. At the first sighting, the line of owners and supporters who had been languishing and chatting among themselves were alert. Every nerve and muscle was taut. Pandemonium broke out. The supporters shouted, screamed, whistled naturally or (if they had false teeth) used metal whistles. Owners advanced, some in a curious crouching gait, staring fixedly ahead, extending the hand with the container of food to its maximum length.

There was a flurry of people and hounds. The hounds had run ten miles because for each there was a meal of sorts as a reward. It might be hard beef, veal, venison or (especially in warm weather) fish.

The premier topic of conversation was Wassie. Could this gingerish beast really be dead?

112

The team from Summit Television had heard it said that someone close to Royalty had hinted that Prince Charles was interested in it and might just drop in. Jonty the Postman recalled Riseley's letter address to this eminent person at Buckingham Palace.

The television coverage was live—and, with Wasdale being a deep little valley among some of the highest mountains in the land—setting up the facilities had cost an eye and a leg. In a fanciful moment, Gerald Twitch-Bell had thought of putting a dish on top of Great Gable. There were technical problems, though, and he would also have to make peace with the conservation groups, with which Lakeland abounded, though Summit Television was sponsoring a *Take a Duster to Lakeland* campaign, a variation on the Best-kept Village idea.

The Wasdalians, by now thoroughly accustomed to the Media, almost queued up to be interviewed by the dishy presenters. Several days before, Simeon had been seen having a wash in a cracked enamel bowl in the back yard. Then he spent hours trying to tame his beard. He appeared before the cameras looking positively civilised. He was amazed how thin and pale the city girls were. "Nay, lass," he said to one of them. "Have a good meal. Next wind will blow you over."

Someone was testing the special loudspeaker system. Simeon's voice boomed across the valley. Everyone cheered.

The emaciated lass asked Isaac to talk about Wasdale mysteries. Overcoming his shyness with strangers, he was soon relating the hoary tale of the days when anyone who died in the valley was buried in Eshd'l (Eskdale).

The body was conveyed there, across the moor, strapped to the back of a fell pony. Inevitably, one pony bolted. It ran off, with the coffin still in place and "they niver knew t'end of it. For all we know, it's still up theer—the skeleton of a hoss wi' a rotting coffin."

The television interviewer paled as he spoke.

She had signed off for a short time when Riseley appeared, ready to claim the President's right to be interviewed about the show. Isaac was talking to Simeon. The wee lassie from the Telly had departed for a cup of tea—or something stronger.

Riseley, who had given the impression of affability, had

113

months of pent-up rage against Isaac to release. Tyson typified the rough-and-ready Lakeland sheep farmer, resistent to change. When he was not invited to the microphone, and Isaac had just signed off, Riseley lost his cool, strode up to the farmer and said, caustically: "I suppose you've been telling tales about me."

There was no obvious change in Isaac's manner, though Simeon recognised in the tightened muscles, the whitening of the sides of his face and the way he lifted the back of his cap and scratched the nape of his neck, his old friend's annoyance. Isaac stood his ground and said nowt. He was rather like a herdwick tup, biding his time to attack.

Major Riseley talked himself into a tantrum. "I've had nothing but trouble with your family since I came here..."

This point demanded an answer, but none came.

"You dalesfolk think you're the lords of creation."

Isaac shifted his weight from one foot to another.

Riseley, seething with anger, lunged towards Isaac and met, in Isaac's fist, the equivalent of a brick wall. Mrs Riseley rushed to her husband's aid, as a dutiful wife must, but managed to wink at Isaac while doing so.

They had not noticed, during Riseley's outburst, that the crowd in the showground had gone quiet. The only sounds to break the stillness had been the occasional bleat of a sheep or yap of a dog. Now there was a thunderous round of clapping.

Said Simeon: "Someone left t'bluddy sound switched on. It's bin relayed half way round t'dale."

Normal Service was resumed, to quote the Media expression. The dishiest presenter confronted Simeon, who told a book-story (a gory episode) of t'Beckside Boggle down Miterdale Valley. "Yon boggle went to sleep on t'settee in a farmhouse. Farmer's wife poured some hot fat over him and killed him."

The television interviewer came close to swooning.

To the collection of strange tales was now added the Wasdale Monster. There was Jonty the Postman, out of uniform, telling the old, old story of how his postbus was attacked and ROYAL MAIL became ROYAL MA. The account was beginning to become a classic.

Major Riseley, nursing an inflamed cheek, was back on duty at the President's tent, which he was now disinclined to leave.

114

His wife's titter had infected the entire field.

Meanwhile, the traditional life of Wasdale Show went on, except that the men now wore colourful plastic showerproof clothing almost like a uniform and clumped about in wellies. As ever, the field was half full of bearded characters, men who might have walked straight from the pages of Thomas Hardy. Some beards were as stiff as scrubbing-brushes. For every tidy beard, three were as much out of control as Russian vine on the vicarage wall.

Prize herdwick tups, as white-faced as clowns and with fleeces in all the glory of show-red, ground their teeth or butted each other through boredom. These noble animals were confined in pens when they would have preferred the open fell. They stood stoically, on legs like those of an oaken table, and tried to ignore all the fuss and blather around them.

When the time came for a herdwick tup to be put on show for judging, a farmer grasped its horns as he would "tak hod" of the handlebars of a bike. The herdwick has a highly efficient braking system. When feeling peevish, it had to be slurred into position. The proud owner placed its feet so they would show off the animal at its best. Next, he was grasping a horn with one hand and fluffing up any crushed wool with the other.

At a family show, the tourists stood out. In the first place, they were gormless when it came to country ways. And in the second, they were always queuing up for refreshments and forever stuffing lollies and ice creams into the faces of their young. This year, there was a third category—men, wearing their tweed suits like uniforms. Now and again you'd come across one of them with a walk-talkie (nowt so common as a mobile phone).

P C Leonard Hoggarth, of the Cumbrian Constabularly, was here. There was nowt special in that. A dozen other policeman had turned up.

"What's up?" asked Isaac.

"Nowt," said the constable.

"It's takking a lot of policeman to deal wi' nowt," persisted Isaac. "Don't say yon Riseley chap has actually got Prince Charles to come to Wasd'l?"

And P C Hoggarth, who was usually very chatty, simply said: "I won't say."

115

The Wasdale collie dogs were the first to pick up the sound of the helicopter. A couple of dozen pairs of ears were tuned to the west. Then there was a scatter of fell sheep, which was unusual. They'd got so used to low-flying jets they nivver stopped grazing while they shot by, like aerial vacuum cleaners, but this sound was different.

What looked at first glance like a red sycamore seed appeared, whirling against the azure blue of a cloudless sky. It resolved itself into a helicopter. The police and the tweedy men stiffened. Some began to jabber into their walkie-talkies. There was a last minute sweep of Jossie Eldin's best meadow as the whirlygig, pillar box red, with silvery highlights where the bright paintwork caught the sun, descended to an uneventful landing.

From the helicopter alighted a smiling little woman.

Henry stepped forward and kissed her. "Grannie," he said, "you're a day late."

As Isaac said, drily: "She'll have read about our Wassie in t'New York papers and she's come to see for hersen."

Mrs Swartz, the former owner of upper Wasdale (with the exception of the Tyson farm) was fussed over by a much-chastened Riseley who, truly, had thought the helicopter had been one of the Queen's flight.

* * *

There was yet more commotion. Owd Jack from Gill Head arrived, hours late, driving his Fordson tractor, creating such a smokescreen you might think the engine ran on peat.

In tow was a home-made trailer from which came a clattering sound, not unlike that made by a restless horse. It must be a late arrival for the livestock section. And, indeed, Jack drove his tractor and trailer to within a few yards of where the judges had been standing, before the helicopter landed.

The thumping sound from the trailer was joined by a new sound: a dull thud, as of horn against wood. It was a herdwicky sound—but much louder than that made when a Wasdale tup,

116

peeved at being held in a small pen, delivered (coolly, unemotionally) some fence-shattering butts with its horns at the perimeters of its prison. It drowned t'sound of helicopter rotors, which were still spinning.

Krump! Several pieces of wood came under violent strain. *Krump! krump!* There was a rending of wood. A few more krumps, each louder than the last, and the trailer burst asunder, revealing yet another Monster.

It was Big. Bold. And Gingery.

Each farmer had appraised it in seconds. It stood perhaps three times as big as your average herdwick tup. Its eyes glowed. The horns were thick and curved, twice as fearsome as the horns of the average bull, let alone sheep.

"Hell, Jack—whatever has ta brought wi' thee?" asked Isaac Tyson.

There was no time for Jack to reply.

A Monsterproof cordon of men appeared round Mrs Swartz, who smiled at all the fuss, not realising she was deputising, in a way, for Princes Charles.

The cordon was not Monsterproof. Wassie—or was it a friend of Wassie?—saw the red helicopter gleaming in the sunlight and made for it with the reckless determination of a Rugby League player about to touch-down at Whitehaven.

Anyone in its path did the sensible thing—and scattered.

Big, hairy, rippling with muscle like a giant wild boar, but with general characteristics like a gurt big herdwick tup, the Monster of Wasdale leapt at its red rival. Horns crashed against shining metal. An enormous dinge appeared on the side of the helicopter.

Mrs Swartz pulled up her tweedy skirt and ran with the others to the sanctuary of a tent. Riseley and the cream of his social connections ran. The only man to stand still was a cameraman from Summit Television, so excited at recording what was happening he followed the progress of Wassie. It was a pity that the technicians who might have recorded the images were running towards photographic infinity.

"What the hell have you done?" demanded Issac from Old Jack.

"How do you mean?"

117

"Thou's taken a smile off everybody's face. And almost wrecked a helicopter."

"It's bin a funny day," said Jack. "When I got out o' bed, I brok a cup an' saucer'."

Isaac laughed, really laughed, for the first time for years. The two friends turned to where they had last seen the Monster.

Said Old Jack: "I found it on t'fell. It was a tup 'at grew from a lamb I had on t'marshes. Summat happened down there. When it came back, I couldn't keep yon tup lamb at home. Kept it in a poultry hut. (He wheezed). And look what it's grown up into. I'd to 'tice it into t'trailer with some turnips."

"Wonderful," said Professor Ock. "An irradiated tup. Nothing like ziss has been seen before. Don't harm it."

"Nay," said Jack, "It's not that special. It's fadder was a big 'un, too."

Most people had no intention of going near it. The Monster of Wasdale, having galloped well beyond the helicopter, savaging a few cars and a tractor on the way, was now returning through the showground.

Its progress might be noted by the way the shrieking crowd scattered and tents collapsed. The loudspeaker system went off the air, the final words being: "There's a bluddy bull loose...."

It was young Jamie Thwaite who tamed Wassie. As the Monster did a bizarre Lap of Honour, leaving the showfield in chaos, the innkeeper's freckled son stood there, cocksure. As though cheated of other prey, the huge animal lumbered towards him.

Jamie didn't try anything fancy, like using his anorak to deflect the Monster's attention. He simply landed it a crack on its nose with a handy balk of wood.

The Monster recoiled, shook its head several times and, with watering eyes and bleeding nose, headed in panic for Wastwater. Dashing into the water, it began to swim across.

Then it vanished from sight.

Some said it simply gave up swimming and sank. It didn't want to face Jamie again. Others claimed they had seen a swirl in the water, as if some other Monster—perhaps a cousin of Nessie— had grabbed it and taken it under.

For days afterwards, the dalesfolk kept their eye on the shores

118

of the lake, including the groves of gorse and ruckle of boulders, but all they found were the ordinary sights of Wasdale—the red-faced, half-dressed courting couple; the picnic party, about to set fire to the district with their primus stove and, one morning, trapped between stones on the lakeshore, a tuft of ginger hair.

Our story ends where it began—with a tuft of hair.

Epilogue

There is a bit of tidying up to do.

Wassie is dead, but not forgotten. The scientists still argue about him. Was he just an extra big herdwick tup? Or a hybrid with savage inclinations? Had he come about through some genetic disturbance? Or was he irradiated by Chernobyl? as the old professor (now head of the Summit Television science bureau) believes.

The Monster industry of Wasdale is doing well, thank you. Below the old hall is a theme park, under a huge plastic dome so that if it rains none of the visitors will get wet. Nor, said Isaac, will they have the pleasure of feeling the wind and rain on their cheeks. Herdwick tups are living behind huge sheets of magnifying glass to make them monster-like. A succession of blood-curdling sounds, like echoes from prehistory, evoke an exciting atmosphere.

How such a project got past the planners we will never know. Except that the manager is Major Riseley, late of the Swartz Trust. A bit of land, well out of sight of the road, was a farewell gift to him by the family.

There's not much of the Old Wasdale left. Some farms are now shops, with fresh farm produce brought in daily by lorry. Gift

119

shops galore are stocked with everything from Monster tea-towels to Monster toothpaste (which has streaks of ginger in the stripes).

Mrs Swartz had offered Wasdale to Henry, who accepted but now said: "No thanks." He and Jane emigrated to Keswick. Henry runs a bookshop which makes a small profit one year and a small loss in the following year. He's just found a publisher for his Wasdale researches, which will have the title *An Introduction to the Study of the Social Life of a Lakeland Dale*. Large sales are not expected. There's a good photograph of the Monster on page 216.

Jane is still doing veterinary work, but now the call sign is "Base to JS." Jane has managed to produce and sustain a lusty child—a boy, who looks just like Henry and whose first word was "Gee!"

Owd Jack died. His former home is tummelling doon. Tony, who married the dark lass from Washolme after getting her into trouble, has been knocked into a reasonable shape by his spirited wife who, in return has made him the proud father of half a dozen bairns.

Our story began with Jonty the Postman. He has retired to a Council flat in Whitehaven. Above the fireplace hangs a mounted postbus hub cap, somewhat dented.

The Swartz Trust is Wasdale plc., owned by Summit Television, who are discouraging local people from using the name Wasdale in their advertisements. There is no active farmer left in the valley. The ground is swamped with species of cattle and sheep bearing strange foreign names.

Some of the more delicate sheep over-winter in a huge shed. People gather on turning-out day. The sheep have been crammed together for so long, they move out and advance up the hillside in a block. Then, realising they are free to move about, the flock disperses.

The Wasdale Monster has not been seen again but, as Isaac Tyson, sheep farmer of Wasdale Head, remarked to Reg, former Editor of the *Cumberland Gazette*, during a rare visit to Wasdale with his wife Mabel: "I reckon t'Monster's still with us."

They shook their heads sadly as day-trippers arrived at the car park near the kirk, to buy Monster Rock, Monster soft toys,

120

Wassie the Monster videos (copyright—Summit Television) and Monster crayoning books for children.

Said Isaac: "I reckon t'Wasdale Monster is getting bigger and stronger by the day. It's called Progress, lad. But it's Exploitation. Media Madness. Souvenir Sickness. Tourist Trivia. Call it what you will. And we can't do a damn thing about it..."

They were looking towards Great Gable at the time. Perhaps it was a trick of the evening light but Isaac swore the old mountain winked at him.

Castleberg Books (Spring, 1996)

North Country Books by W R Mitchell

The Lost Shanties of Ribblehead

This is a distillation of many years of research into the temporary hut-settlements built during the construction of the Settle-Carlisle (1869-76). It tells of domestic and social life of the navvies and their families, the work of railway missionaries and the methods used by local policemen. The backdrop to all this activity is Ribblehead viaduct and the tunnel driven through Blea Moor. Foreword by Peter Caldwell, one of the archaeologists who have recently studied the Batty Moss navvy settlements.

A New Paperback. ISBN: 1 871064 83 X £5.99

Ribblehead Re-born

Reprint of a well-illustrated account of the history, folklore, design, construction and survival of a stupendous piece of Victorian railway engineering. It was first issued in 1992, on the completion of a restoration costing £3 million and had the collaboration of A P Freschini (resident engineer) and Geoff Bounds (Project Manager, Settle-Carlisle).

96 pages. ISBN: 871064 70 8 £5.60

The Men who Made the Settle-Carlisle
Edited version of three former 'Castleberg' titles—about Shanty Life, How they Built the fell-top railway and Footplate Tales.
120 pages. ISBN: 1 871064 86 4   £5.99

Dent: the Highest Mainline Station in England
Cecil Sanderson, a wartime Stationmaster, who battled with a blizzard on the night his son was born, and Jack Sedgwick, the signalman who sometimes tickled trout in the beck on his way to work, are among those featured in this entrancing book.
ISBN: 1 871064 93 7   £5.99

Miss Harriet Martineau's Guide to Windermere (1854)
This facsimile reproduction of a scarce old booklet gives an insight into mid-nineteenth century life in the Windermere district and is complete with a directory.
Over 100 pages. ISBN: 1871064 88 0   £5.60

Mr Elgar and Dr Buck
A fifty year long friendship between the famous composer and a Dales doctor. Many illustrations, including facsimile pages from Elgarian letters. Foreword by Lady Barbirolli.
122 pages. ISBN: 1 871064 05 8   £5.60

The Lost Village of Stocks-in-Bowland
Reprint of the only book relating to life in the upper Hodder Valley before and during the construction of Stocks Reservoir. Based on taped interviews with those who recall those eventful days.
ISBN: 1 871064 90 2   £5.60

Stocks Re-visited
A second book about Stocks Reservoir, containing more facts and tales from the 'lost village'.
ISBN: 1 871064 96 1   £5.60

The Lost Village of Mardale (Haweswater)
Best-selling book about Old Mardale and how an old-established Lakeland community came to an end when Manchester flooded the valley. Based largely on first-hand accounts of the transition.
ISBN: 1 871064 92 9   £5.99

Castleberg Bargains

Letters from the Lakes

Foreword by Hunter Davies

Wordsworthian daffodils, Beatrix Potter's fascination with Lakeland farming, Wasdale Walls, Ponies of Heltondale, Sphinx and Napes Needle, Bitterns and Otters, what lies Back o' Skiddaw — and much else.

Paperback 172 pages. ISBN: 1 871064 94 5 ~~£5.99~~ **Now £3.00**

Letters from the Dales

A unique record of everyday life in the Dales. The author writes with candour and humour about old-time dances, drystone walls, hand-knitting, tewits and ring ouzels, sheep and shepherds, potholers, Irish haytimers, the Settle-Carlisle Railway — and much else.

Paperback 168 pages. ISBN: 1 871064 99 6 ~~£5.99~~ **Now £3.00**

A Passion for Puffins

The author goes in search of our favourite seabird from the cliffs of his native Yorkshire, to remote parts of Scotland and Iceland and with a footfall beyond the Arctic Circle.

Colour cover and thirty line illustrations by David Binns, one of the best-known wildlife artists in Britain.

120 pages. ISBN: 1 871064 97 X

~~£5.99~~ **Now only £1.99 (plus 60p post)**

drawing by Richard Bancroft

Life and Traditions of the Ribble Valley

Read about the lost islands of the Ribble, whistling deer, silver mines, a famous hymn-tune, witches, and treacle-and-oatmeal weavers among other lively tales. The river itself, Old Man Ribble, forms the principal theme.

ISBN 1 871064 98 8 ~~£5.99~~ **Now £3.00**

Ingleborough: The Big Blue Hill

Ingleborough, the most popular hill in Yorkshire, has a book to itself, with sections on The Natural Scene, History, Folklore, Farming, Early Tourism and Caving. Also an account of Seven Ways up Ingleborough.

Paperback 120 pages   ISBN: 1 871064 87 2 ~~£5.99~~ **Now £3.00**

Hotfoot to Haworth

The absorbing story of pilgrimages to the shrine of the Bronte family, from the arrival of the Duke of Devonshire with a brace of grouse to the mass invasion of today. 96 pages.

ISBN: 1 871064 75 9 ~~£4.99~~ **Now £3.00**